William the Hedgehog Boy

William the Hedgehog Boy

How one incident
can change everything

Robert A. Brown

Matador
9 Priory Business Park,
Wistow Road, Kibworth Beauchamp,
Leicestershire. LE8 0RX
Tel: 0116 279 2299
Email: books@troubador.co.uk
Web: www.troubador.co.uk/matador
Twitter: @matadorbooks

ISBN 978 1788037 471

British Library Cataloguing in Publication Data.
A catalogue record for this book is available from the British Library.

Printed and bound in the UK by TJ International, Padstow, Cornwall
Typeset in 12pt Baskerville by Troubador Publishing Ltd, Leicester, UK

Matador is an imprint of Troubador Publishing Ltd

My Karon, without whom this book may never have been finished. For her patience, for the countless proof readings, the critical advice, all the support and believing in me.

For Chubby (the first hedgehog we released into our garden), with grateful thanks for sticking around and inspiring me to learn more about these amazing animals.

For Chris Lee, my writing buddy, whose ideas and delightful pen and ink drawings and front cover design helped to bring my characters to life.

Snuffles Rescue Centre for their commitment, care and dedication on a daily basis to save our hedgehogs. Also for giving me permission to use some of their resources and information sheets.

The army of people who work tirelessly supporting our endangered wildlife so that future generations of children can also be inspired.

The team at Matador whose skill and professionalism turned my manuscript into the book you are now reading.

Contents

Chapter 1

To The Rescue

Morning, Saturday October 14th

"But why did you have to marry *him*, Mum?" said William, putting a heavy emphasis upon *him*. "*He's* nothing like my real dad?"

"When your father was killed in that accident, I thought my life was over; I didn't know how I could carry on." William was listening carefully now. He remembered how often he had heard his mum crying in her bedroom at night. It seemed to him that the whole house was sad. In every room there were photos of his dad, reminding them both of what they had lost.

His mum continued, "You must remember Nan and Grandad visiting us all the time to try and help me, and you going to stay with them during the school holidays?"

"Yes I remember, I used to love playing with Poppy; I really wanted to have a puppy but you wouldn't let me because we would have to leave it on its own all day."

"Well, after a while, I got to know David at work and he was really kind to me. He has really helped me to move on."

"But Mum, I thought you really loved Dad. How can you just forget about him?"

"William, you must never think that. I will never forget your dad. I think about him every day, but we have to move on. We cannot spend the rest of our lives being unhappy, can we? Your dad wouldn't want that, would he?"

William sat quietly, thinking about what his mum had said. He could see that his dad wouldn't want them to be unhappy forever. He had always been laughing and joking.

"William, I thought you liked David too, that's why I agreed to marry him. I was just so lonely and I wanted us to be a family again."

William's mind went back to the recent wedding; it had rained all day, which he felt was a bad omen. His mum had become Mrs Margaret Harrison. His name had been changed too; from that day on he was to be known as William Harrison, which was something he was still getting used to.

"At least since we've moved here you've got a nice big bedroom, with a desk for your computer and games," she added, trying to think of something positive to say to cheer him up.

"But Mum, David is so strict and serious; I hate it when he tells me off and sends me to my room. I get scared when he is mad with me."

"I know son, it will take us all a while to get used to each other; I know he really cares about us both, so just give him a little time, please."

"Why should I? He's not my real dad!" William blurted out, jumping to his feet and rushing towards the back door, tears stinging his eyes as he grabbed his coat before slamming the door behind him. Once he was outside, he realised that he should never have said that to his mum. The anger had been building up inside him and it just came out. She would be really upset… again.

He hurried past the garage and down the garden path, and then just as he approached the orchard he could hear the sound of boys laughing. He leant over and quietly lifted the latch on the gate and squeezed through the tiny gap. He daren't open it fully in case it squeaked and alerted whoever it was making the noise. Creeping forwards along the path he dodged behind the trunk of an apple tree and peered around the side. His heart was racing as he spotted several boys with their backs towards him. They were peering at the ground and laughing. They were too busy to notice him as he crept forward keeping low and out of sight. Finally, he stopped behind the trunk of a thick old apple tree. He was now only ten metres from the group. He recognised them immediately.

It was the boys from school, the ones in his class, who were always horrid to him, calling him 'Lippy' because of the scar on his top lip. Fortunately, they still hadn't seen him. Tommy Smithers was poking something with a stick and Col' and Johnno were throwing stones and apples at whatever it was on the ground. They were all laughing. He knew how cruel they could be and he suspected something was being hurt. He knew he should do something, but what could he do alone? Looking around he saw a thick branch lying in the wet grass about a metre away. He crouched down, reached out and grabbed it with both hands. He could feel one of his terrible rages building up inside him because of all the times they'd picked on him at school. He turned, lifting the branch above his head and charged at them, screaming at the top of his voice, "Aaaaaahh'll have you!"

The boys were so startled by this mad person screaming at them that they just ran. They didn't stop until they reached the gap in the hedge and began squeezing through as quickly as they could. Tommy turned and saw that it was William waving his stick at them and he sneered, "You wait Lippy, we'll get you for this."

Looking down, William was amazed to see a hedgehog curled up into a tight ball with stones and apples lying around it. He reached down and gently picked it up, wrapping it in his coat to prevent the spines pricking his hands. A bright red smear of blood smudged his sleeve. The poor hedgehog was obviously badly injured. William began running as if his life depended upon it. He didn't bother to tell his mum back at the house. He decided that if he stopped it might be too late. He had to try and save this poor animal even if he had to run all the way to the vets.

Chapter 2

How I Got My Name

Early evening, Saturday October 14th

A bright light was dazzling me, making my eyes sting. I closed them again and tried to move, but I couldn't. Something wasn't right. In fact it was very wrong. I was feeling so sleepy; I just couldn't keep my eyes open. What has happened to me? I forced myself to try and remember. Vague memories started coming back to me through the thick fog in my mind. I remember being in an orchard and some boys were climbing the trees and throwing sticks to try and get the apples down. I didn't think they had seen me, until suddenly one called out. Then, they ran over and started poking me with a branch and throwing stones at me. I remember curling up into a ball to protect myself. I was helpless and I really thought that I was about to die...

Just then, I heard a voice and I strained to listen.

"She's waking up. The anaesthetic must be wearing off. Do you think she'll pull through?" asked a female voice anxiously.

"She should do, if she gets over the operation okay, but she'll need a lot of care over the next few days. Best let her rest now, leave the drip in and pop in every few minutes to check on her," replied a man's voice.

Pull through! What did they mean *pull through*? I must have been badly hurt by those boys; what's an operation? What is going on? What has happened to me? I felt very woozy and I must have drifted off to sleep again…

Sometime later, as my mind began to clear, I could tell things were not right. My legs felt weak, I had a strange taste in my mouth and my jaw hurt… a lot.

"Mr Wilson," called out the female voice, "she's waking up; should I give her a liquid feed?"

"Yes, that should be fine Sue," Mr Wilson replied, "no solids, just a sugar solution with two milligrams of the usual post-op antibiotics. We don't want that wound becoming infected." He paused and then continued, "First though, I suggest you tell her friend the news; he's been in the waiting room for hours. You can let him watch you if you like."

"That's a good idea, he can watch whilst I prepare the mixture," she said.

I looked around and discovered that I was in a box, lined with soft green material. I could hear a dog yapping nearby and I tried to curl into a ball but my body wouldn't obey me. My jaw was throbbing really painfully now, and my mouth felt as if I had been eating holly leaves. The lady called Sue returned and I could just make out that she was wearing a green top. She had short blonde hair and she was smiling.

"This way William, the poor thing is in this box; my name is Sue by the way. She is still very sleepy after her operation. It was really lucky that you saved her and brought her here straight away. If you hadn't, we don't think she would have made it."

A boy's head appeared over the side of the box and he looked down on me. He had a very worried look on his face.

"Now, I'm just going to give her a few drops from this syringe every couple of minutes so that we don't choke her or make her sick," she said, as she gently lifted my head and carefully placed the syringe in between my lips. I recognised that the boy called William was the same one who rescued me in my nightmare. He was watching her very closely as she slowly dribbled the liquid into my mouth. I noticed that he had brown eyes and his short, dark brown hair was parted on the side. There was a big scar between his top lip and his nose, which made his lip curve in a way I'd not seen before. Not that I'd seen many humans before and certainly not this close up.

After watching her very closely for a few moments the boy asked, "Can I do that? I'd love to feed her."

"Oh no, I don't think so. I'm sure Mr Wilson would be cross with me…"

"Cross with you for what?" enquired Mr Wilson as he entered the room.

Startled, Sue became flustered as she said, "Oh, oh, I didn't see you come in Mr Wilson. William here has asked if he can feed her and I was just explaining to him that he couldn't as the hedgehog is still terribly weak."

"Do you really think you could do it William?" asked the vet. "It must be done very carefully and recorded on that sheet attached to her box."

"I think so, please let me help her," pleaded William.

"What about your parents, they must be wondering where you are? You cannot stay here as surgery closes at eight and you've been here for ages already."

"It's okay; I already called my mum, so she knows where I am. I'll call her again just to make sure it's all right. Oh please let me take care of her."

"William, it's already well past tea-time, you must be starving; it's dark now, where do you live?" Mr Wilson asked.

"18, Stenmore Road," William replied. "Don't worry, I'm not hungry and I can walk it if my stepfather can't pick me up."

"Stenmore Road! That's at least two miles away, on the far side of the village. Did you run all that way to bring her here?"

"I had to, I could tell that she was badly injured and my stepfather had gone to the match."

"Well, this has to be the luckiest hedgehog in England. I think we should call her 'Lucky', how does that sound William?"

"Lucky," William said quietly to himself as he thought about it, "yes, Lucky sounds perfect."

"Good, now that's sorted," Mr Wilson said before continuing, "you must ring your parents and see if it's possible for them to pick you up later. Then, you can feed Lucky, after you've watched Sue do it a couple more times. Okay, now, I've got some poorly animals waiting for me," and with that he turned and went back into his consulting room.

"Now you can do it William, you have to pick her up very carefully and let her lick the drops of solution off the end of the syringe," said Sue. "Then we record how much she has had on this chart."

William put on the thick leather gloves and lifted me very gently, placing the nozzle of the syringe against my lips. He talked to me all the time he was holding me. His voice sounded soft and it made me feel safe.

Later, when his stepfather arrived to collect him, William came over to my box and said, "Now Lucky, you get some rest and I'll come back on Monday, after school, and feed you again."

William kept his promise and did most of my

feeding over the next few afternoons. He would come straight from school to see how I was doing and to feed me. In fact, he did such a great job that Mr Wilson agreed to let him take me home to look after me, over the half-term holiday. He gave him detailed instructions about how to care for me, and that was how I got to know William and how I got the name 'Lucky'.

Chapter 3

Getting To Know William

Half-Term Week, October 23rd – 27th

Over the next week William looked after me very well. He talked to me all the time and I learned all about his life.

One morning, William told me how horrible some of the children were at school. It seems that there is a group of boys that pick on him and call him 'Lippy'. He explained that he'd been born with a split in his top lip, and that he'd had an operation to fix it, just like me. These were the same boys who had been throwing stones at me. He laughed when he realised that we had something in common. I too had a swollen lip and my jaw was not straight. He explained that he had no brothers or sisters to play with and no friends at school and so he felt very lonely.

One afternoon, he decided to take me outside in my cardboard box, to get some fresh air. He collected some worms, slugs and beetles from the vegetable patch for me to eat. They tasted so much better than the cat food he had been feeding me.

He put on his thick gloves before lifting me out of the box and placing me on the grass. I sniffed the air and felt free again. Suddenly, a black dog called Jessy came into the garden. William laughed when I curled up into a ball as the dog started sniffing around me and she'd yelped when my spines pricked her nose.

Chapter 4

William Gets Some Very Bad News

Morning, Saturday October 28th

During the past week I had visited Mr Wilson the vet for check-ups a couple of times. Each day my jaw was feeling less painful. I had been eating the cat food that William's mum had bought for me for a few days now. It certainly tasted better than it looked. It smelled really strange to my sensitive nose. It was definitely not as tasty as my favourites, the slippery worms and crunchy beetles that William gave me.

On this particular Saturday morning William put me into a new cardboard box, with a soft towel on the bottom. He was getting me ready for my next visit to see Mr Wilson, the vet. When we entered the Veterinary Centre we were met by the familiar smell of disinfectant. As we were waiting for our turn to be seen, from inside my box I could hear a dog whining pitifully. I could tell it was very scared and wanted to run away. I could hear his owner trying to reassure him by saying over and over again, 'Shush Rocky, there's a good boy.'

Just then, my nose picked up a new smell. I guessed that the dog had relieved itself on the floor. I scrambled up the side of the box and peeped over the side to watch the commotion as the lady behind the desk came rushing over. The owner was now saying sorry to her and telling the dog off. The woman, who was wearing a green top and trousers, put on some yellow gloves and quickly cleared up the mess. It wasn't long before William and his stepdad stood up and carried me into the consulting room where Mr Wilson was waiting.

Mr Wilson checked me over very thoroughly, putting something into his ears to listen to my chest. Then he placed me on some scales and weighed me. He nodded when he looked at the display before finally lifting me up and looking straight at my face.

He turned to William and said, "Well young man, you've done a wonderful job with her. You should be very proud of yourself. The jawbone is setting really well and she is now fully recovered. I'm afraid she won't win any prizes for her looks. She'll always have a crooked jaw, but that doesn't seem to affect her eating at all." He gently lowered me back into my box before adding, "She's also putting on weight which is essential if she is to be fit for her winter hibernation."

"What is hibernation?" asked William anxiously.

"Well William, hedgehogs are amazing creatures

that have evolved over thousands of years to survive the winter by going into a deep sleep. When the weather turns cold and frosty, the worms and insects they like to eat burrow deep into the ground or hide in shelters where the hedgehogs cannot find them. The hedgehogs would starve to death. So instead hedgehogs try to put on weight and build up their fat reserves. Then, when they begin their deep sleep they slow down their breathing rate and heart rate so that they use very little energy. This enables them to sleep through the coldest months of winter before they wake up again in the spring. To do this they need to find a safe, warm cosy den if they are to survive."

"Does that mean I can't keep her?" William asked anxiously.

Mr Wilson took a deep breath, before answering in a softer, gentler tone, "I know that Lucky here has become your friend William, and you see her as a pet, but you must remember that she is a wild animal. She needs her freedom now. She needs time to find a suitable den so that she can hibernate and survive the winter."

William's stepdad said, "So you see William, we need to take Lucky home and let her go, perhaps in the orchard. Then she can learn to look after herself again and put enough weight on to be ready for the winter…"

I was not sure if I was ready to face the big wide world yet, particularly after the last time. Then I saw William's face changing; it sort of screwed up and his lips started trembling, his eyes filled with water and tears began running down his cheeks.

"Please let me keep her, you know I can look after her and keep her safe," begged William, pulling on his stepdad's coat, "PLEEEASE."

"Now that's enough William," said his stepdad sharply, "Mr Wilson has been very kind, he's a busy man and you don't want to let yourself down by crying in front of him."

Mr Wilson put his hand on William's shoulder and said, "It's understandable to get upset about animals, it shows how much you care. However, she really will be better off when she's free again. That is how hedgehogs are meant to live."

"Please let me keep her a little longer," William said. "I don't have to go to school next Monday or Tuesday because of teacher training. I could help her to get used to being outside again."

Mr Wilson thought for a moment before suggesting, "That's a good idea William. I tell you what; you know how you've been feeding her cat food and a few worms for a while now. Well, I suggest that you release her early next week, but make sure you

put a little cat food out for her at night. In that way you can be sure she won't go hungry."

William couldn't speak; he just kept looking down at his feet. After a few moments, Mr Wilson added, "Also, how would you like to help my wife with the animals in the Rescue Centre on Saturday mornings? You've done such a good job with Lucky and she needs a reliable assistant. You would be able to learn how to look after some of the other animals. We could give you a trial to see how it goes. Now what do you say?"

William bunched his hands into fists and rubbed his eyes and stopped sobbing before he replied, "That would be great thanks, and thank you for helping Lucky get better."

Back on the way home, his stepdad, David, was telling William what a good job he'd done to help me get better, and that he was proud of him. William just sat in silence staring down at me in my box; he was too upset to speak…

I too was thinking about my freedom; what if those boys find me again? What if I can't find my den? What if I cannot find enough juicy worms, sticky slugs and crunchy beetles to eat?

Soon the car turned into the driveway and came

to a stop. There was a brief silence until William's stepdad said, "Come on young man, let's go and see your mum and tell her the news."

Chapter 5

Free Again

Late afternoon, Tuesday October 31st

When David, William's stepdad, returned from work he told William that it was time for me to be released into the orchard. William tried to argue but he was reminded that Mr Wilson had said that it was against the law to keep wild animals as pets. You have to have a proper licence like the Rescue Centre.

So, a little while later, the family gathered in the orchard. The grass was long and wet so they were all wearing their wellies. It was a crisp, late autumn afternoon. It would soon be dark. The pale moon was already visible. The wind had swept the leaves up against the foot of the hawthorn hedge, like a brown and gold scarf.

William was wearing the thick gardening gloves he always wore when handling me. They protected him from my five thousand prickly spines, whenever he lifted me out of the box…

I could sense how upset he was as he gently lifted me out of the box. I peeped between his fingers and saw that we were in the orchard. I sniffed the cold air using my sensitive nose as he gently placed me on the grass.

"Take care, I'll miss you; you are my only real friend," he whispered as he squatted beside me and said, "Be lucky."

I nuzzled his gloved hand, sniffed the air once more and decided to make for the hawthorn hedge. I hoisted up the soft, brown fur that skirts the bottom edge of my body and scuttled away on my stubby legs. Once I'd reached the hedge, I stopped and turned to look back. The family were all watching me. I think William's mum had something in her eyes as she was dabbing them with a handkerchief. William's stepdad put his arm around her shoulders and I heard him say, "Come on, let's get inside, it's cold out here and we all need a hot drink." They both turned and began walking back towards the gate. It seemed a long time before William moved anywhere. I could see him standing there, all alone, watching me, my empty box in his hands.

Chapter 6

Monsters In The Garden

Early evening on Tuesday October 31st

I moved off into the hedgerow, sniffing the air every few seconds. Any strong scents could spell danger. I wanted to get away from that orchard as quickly as possible, in case those boys returned. Most of all I wanted to get back to my home where I knew I would be safe. There should be plenty of tasty, wriggly worms and crunchy beetles to eat in the vegetable patch.

I scurried around the edge of the orchard before squeezing through a gap in the hedge, using the familiar route back to my den. I could see the yellow pools of light shining out from the windows of the houses. I paused for a moment and wondered what William might be doing. I could imagine him in the kitchen, getting some food for me out of the large, cold white box, or up in his bedroom tapping away with his fingers on that machine.

William had saved my life! He'd always been kind to me. I hoped I would get to see him again sometime. Then I remembered, *Humans are big, noisy and dangerous.* I had already discovered how dangerous they could be during the daytime. My crooked jaw was a daily reminder of just how dangerous! I scuttled along the path, my senses on full alert and my spines standing out in case of a sudden attack.

I reached the wide path that led to the road where the noisy machines rushed by with their dazzling lights. They are really frightening, and our mum had warned us 'hoglets' to stay away from roads. Following her advice, I kept going past William's neighbour's gateway. This was where the black dog lived. I picked up her strong smell with my sensitive nose. She had almost scared me to death when she began sniffing around me. It was a good job that I could curl up into a ball with my needle-sharp spines sticking out. I am lucky to have my prickly spines.

Pausing for a moment, I remembered how upset William had been as he whispered to me, "Take care my friend, be lucky." I moved on trying to avoid being seen by sticking close to the low garden wall to keep out of the light cast by the lamppost.

'Nearly there now,' I thought to myself, trying to calm my nerves down.

Anxiously, I kept sniffing the air, my nerves tingling as I crept up the driveway, keeping to the shadows as I approached the house. I would soon be home at last. I began to relax a little and began thinking about sorting out my cosy den under the shed. Once I had checked it out and made it nice and warm with some fresh leaves, I would go and explore the vegetable patch. I was sure to get a good feed there…

"Shweeeeeeh!" I squealed. I froze to the spot in terror. There was the most terrifying monster, staring straight at me. It had a round, orange face, bright yellow eyes and the sharpest jagged teeth I'd ever seen. My brain went into overdrive trying to decide what to do. Had it seen me? Could I make a run for it? Should I curl up into a ball and wait for the attack? After squealing like that, the monster was sure to have heard me.

I curled up into a really tight ball, sticking my sharp spines straight out to fend off the creature. My heart was thumping so loudly I was sure the hideous monster would hear it too. I held my breath as I squeezed my eyes shut expecting to feel the hot, stinking breath of the creature at any second, as it prepared to devour me. I waited to feel the pain as it attacked me with those huge teeth. I couldn't move a muscle; I listened, not wanting to make a sound…

There was total silence; there was no snarl, no roar, no bark, no running steps on the path, no heavy breathing, just silence.

Perhaps the monster hadn't heard me after all. I'd never seen anything like it before. I tried to remember if I'd noticed any ears, but all I could picture were those terrifying eyes and huge, pointed teeth. Maybe it hadn't seen me after all. I needed to move, to get away, quickly, before it spotted me. I tried to picture the rest of the route to my den. Just around the corner of the house it was dark, but I could see the light from the windows flooding the path that led towards my home and safety. I told myself, *think, if you panic you're dead!* I took a deep breath, trying to calm down and work out what to do…

Right, this is the plan, uncurl and run as fast you can into the dark patch by the wall. Stop, wait and listen, if the monster chases after me I must roll up tight, stick out my spines and fight for my life! If the monster doesn't attack, then I can try to creep slowly into the bushes, and make for my den and safety.

I uncurled out of my ball and, without a glance towards the monster, I ran as fast as I could into the dark space by the wall. Once there, I waited, straining my ears, certain that I would hear the sound of the monster coming after me.

My chest was heaving as I gulped in the cool air…

Not a sound could be heard in the still night. Then suddenly, 'whoo hoo hoo' – an owl startled me as it hooted from the trees close by. I was so jittery that I almost squealed again. I took a deep breath as I paused to rehearse how to put the second part of the plan into action. *Firstly, I would need to find some cover in the bushes… Then, hoist up my underskirt to make sure that the dry leaves don't catch on my spines because the rustling sound could alert the monster. Finally, if the monster doesn't attack me, use the bushes for cover, to creep towards my home under the shed…*

Taking a deep breath, I broke from cover and raced towards the first low bush. The moonlight was casting spidery shadows through the thin leafless branches. I hesitated, waiting for an attack and then I crept forwards very slowly, and quietly, carefully placing each foot to avoid any sticks or twigs that might alert the fiendish creature. It was a route that I had used many times before. I must have still been holding my breath because I suddenly let out a gasp, "Phew! That was lucky."

Chapter 7

Monsters Everywhere

Later on Tuesday Night, October 31st

I began to relax as I continued on my way towards the shed and a millipede wandered into my path. Yummy! Two bites, it tasted so good, although those legs tickled a bit. As I got closer to my den under the shed I sensed that something was wrong. My spines stood up, what was it? I peered into the gloom, looking to see if it was another monster. When I inhaled to take several deep sniffs my nose picked out a strange odour. There was an earthy smell that was different from the familiar musty smell of the shed. I took several more sniffs, testing the air, and sure enough the smell became stronger as I moved closer to the entrance hole. With my senses now on full alert and my spines standing up along my back I wondered what fearful creature had moved into my den. *What if one of those horrible monsters has moved in?*

My mother had warned us about foxes, 'like big brown dogs' she'd said, although I have never seen one. The most dangerous animals of all are the large black and white 'Snufflers'. She told us to keep away from them at all costs. They lived in the woods, in underground tunnels, and only came out when the sun went down. She told us that they had long, sharp claws for digging their tunnels and they would use them to tear us apart if they were hungry. I considered my choices? *If I entered the dark hole under the shed I might be entering the lair of another terrifying monster. Or, I could sit and wait outside in the cold night air feeling increasingly hungry. Or maybe I should try to find a new den.*

I was feeling tired, very hungry, and it was getting colder. I needed to sort out my nest and then get some sleep. I decided to wait.

Within a few moments I heard a rustling sound coming from under the shed.

I pressed myself back into the shadows, behind some plant pots. They were stacked in tall towers at the side of the shed. I knew the humans from the house used them for flowers. The creature, whatever it was, was now at the entrance, and from my position I could just make out its nose as it twitched. It was testing the air, perhaps it could smell me. Just then a black, beady eye came into view scanning ahead. I recognised it instantly. It was another hedgehog! Angry thoughts raged through my brain…

'*This is my den. How dare this creature be using my den? I got there first. I have to get rid of it. I'll kill it if I have to!*'

I waited for the moment to attack as the beast

moved out into the open. As soon as it did I launched myself forwards, charging head down, aiming to strike first. I wanted to get my nose underneath the beast and flip it onto its back. I rammed into it, taking it completely off guard, my nose smashing through the softer fur of his belly. Then I braced my legs and, using all my strength, I used my nose to lift him off his feet. He squealed loudly with shock and was starting to topple over onto his side.

He staggered to his right and managed to stay on his feet. I lunged at him again, but this time he was ready for me. He dodged to his left so that I only managed a glancing blow against his side. Our prickly spines clashed against each other. I stopped my charge and spun around and for the first time I saw the size of my opponent. He was enormous, twice my size, with a much bigger head and longer nose. His body was bulky, covered in long spines and his tiny, black beady eyes were boring into mine. Those eyes made it perfectly clear to me that this particular monster was prepared to fight to the death!

We circled, warily, nose to nose, first one way and then the other. We were both breathing heavily, each seeking an opening for an attack. Looking straight into his eyes, I snarled at him, "What are you doing in my den?"

"Your den," he snorted, "I found it, I have been

here for ages and now I'm going to keep it. First though, I am going to kill you." At this point he feinted as if to go right and I jumped sideways to counter his move. However, he doubled back to the left and lunged at my now exposed right flank. I felt his nose and head crunching into my ribs. I felt my breath exploding out of me. My feet were leaving the floor as he lifted me upwards. I was in big trouble. If I rolled onto my back, my soft belly would be exposed. I could sense the triumphant gleam in his eyes as he snorted, "Now I have you."

This is it I thought; *he is going to kill me!*

Thinking quickly, instead of trying to resist the creature because he was too strong, I brought my feet and claws tight into my chest and curled up tightly into a ball. This enabled me to roll over out of the way until I could spring back onto my feet. Then I spun around to face him again.

"Smart move, you little beggar, but I haven't finished with you yet!" he snarled.

I had to escape before this brute finished me off; but how? He pressed his head against mine and began pushing me backwards. It was hopeless; he was so much bigger, heavier and stronger than me. My claws couldn't get any grip on the smooth concrete slabs at the side of the shed. He shoved harder and my body began sliding backwards. I realised that he was aiming to pin me against the shed wall. He was going to crush me…

I adjusted my position, squatting low with my legs coiled beneath me. I felt his body tense up for the final, body-crushing shove. Suddenly, I stopped resisting and sprang out of his way. His bulky body rushed past me and his speed kept him going until his snout smashed into the tower of pots. The pots toppled over, raining down on his back. He shook himself as if he was confused and couldn't believe what had just happened.

This was my chance to escape. I ran for my life. I raced past the shed, past the vegetable patch and up to the fence on the opposite side of the garden.

I paused, breathing heavily, gulping in air, pain shooting through my ribs with each breath. There was the strong bitter taste of blood in my mouth and my injured jaw was throbbing really painfully again. *Was I badly injured? Was I going to die from that thumping blow?*

Although my battered body needed to rest I still had to escape from this garden of monsters. At least the brute was nowhere to be seen and I certainly wasn't about to wait for him to follow me. A stabbing pain knifed through my ribs which caused me to whimper. I began shuffling along the fence desperately searching for a hole so that I could get away from this terrifying place.

Luckily I found a small gap between a rotten wooden board and the soil and I began digging with my powerful claws. Soon the gap was just big enough for me to be able to squeeze through. It was definitely too small for that massive brute to follow me. I squeezed through, finding myself in another garden.

Stabbing pains kept slicing through my chest, making it hard to breathe, reminding me that I was badly injured. Standing still, I sniffed the air, testing for more strange smells that could mean that there were more monsters about. I listened carefully, in case the brute was following me. Just then the owl hooted again. Perhaps it had been watching all the time and it seemed to say, "Whoo hoo hoo, lucky you."

Chapter 8
Letting Me Go

Meanwhile, in the orchard at that time, Tuesday October 31st

William stood alone watching Lucky until she disappeared from sight in the hedgerow. A great sadness swept over him like a wet blanket. He felt so wretched. *'Why does everything that I love and care for have to go away?'* he thought. Despite what Mr Wilson had said, he knew that he was unlikely to see Lucky ever again. He shuddered in the chilly air as he turned to go back towards the house. In a nearby tree an owl called, "Whoo hoo hoo."

Back at the house, he couldn't face talking to his stepdad and mum, so he quickly removed his coat and wellingtons and went straight up to his bedroom. He could smell the sweet, tempting aroma of the hot chocolate they were drinking. Up in his bedroom, William picked up a photo frame off his bedside table and sat disconsolately on the edge of his bed, his shoulders slumped down. Holding the frame in both hands he stared down at the picture. The photo had been taken by his mum and it showed him holding Lucky with his thick leather gloves. He was smiling straight into the camera. He loved that photo, he had been so happy then and now, as the tears ran down his cheeks, he felt so miserable.

Just then there was a quiet knock on the door.

"William, are you okay? Can I come in please?" asked his mum softly. "I've brought you some hot chocolate." Not waiting for his reply she entered the room and placed the steaming mug onto his bedside table.

She sat down beside him on the edge of his bed and put her arm around him to hold him close to her. William liked that, it made him feel better, he felt safe and that she really cared about him.

"Listen son, I know you are really upset about not being able to keep Lucky, but if you put some food out for her like Mr Wilson said, you might get to see her again. What do you think?"

William stopped sniffling and wiped his nose with his sleeve before replying, "Mr Wilson *actually* said that Lucky might *need* the food, as she might not find enough on her own."

"So, what are you doing up here? She might be starving and relying on you. You should be putting some food out for her," his mum said, hoping that

William would cheer up at the thought of helping Lucky. William didn't move, so she tried again. "David also mentioned that Mr Wilson had offered you the chance to help out in the Animal Rescue Centre on Saturdays."

"Yes, he did," said William.

"That sounds like great fun. You will be able to learn about caring for some other animals, not just hedgehogs." She paused before continuing, "He'd only want someone who was reliable and good with the animals though. Are you sure you're up to it?"

"Oh yes, I think so," said William reaching for the mug and taking a sip, loving its sweet milky taste. "Thanks for the hot chocolate Mum, I'll drink this and then come down and put some food out for Lucky." He replaced the mug on his bedside table before giving her a big hug...

Later in the kitchen, William opened a tin of chicken-flavoured cat food and put it in the same dish that he'd used to feed Lucky when he had been nursing her. It smelled disgusting. He took the dish outside and placed it on the path by the back door. He also rinsed out the water dish and put some fresh water out for her as Mr Wilson had told him to do.

He made sure he could still see the dishes from the kitchen window so that he could keep checking if Lucky came along. It was completely dark now and he wondered what she was doing and where she might be. He hoped she was warm and safe in her home. After tea, William couldn't settle to watch television. His mum was watching one of her favourite programmes in which families and neighbours are rowing and fighting all the time. He didn't feel like starting his new library book as it was a sad book about a puppy that had been abandoned. He couldn't stop thinking about Lucky.

Every few minutes he got up to peek through the window to see if the food had been touched. Eventually, his mum pointed out that it was time to get ready for bed so, after saying good night, he gave his mum and stepdad a hug before having one final check. The food remained untouched and there was no sign of Lucky. He felt really disappointed as he began to trudge up the stairs. As he stepped onto the third step from the bottom it creaked loudly. '*I must remember that,*' he thought. He continued moving upwards, checking the other boards and making a mental note for his route later in the night.

He undressed, carefully so that he would be able to put his slippers on in the dark. His slippers were essential as these would be quietest. He put on his pyjamas, went into the bathroom and brushed his teeth before getting into bed. All was ready…

That night William went to sleep clutching the photo of him holding Lucky in his leather gloves.

Chapter 9

William Has A Plan

Very early morning, Wednesday November 1st

William woke up very early the next morning and noticed that it was still dark outside. Looking at the alarm clock on the bedside table he saw that it was 4.45am. He quietly got out of bed, wriggled his feet into his slippers and, still in his pyjamas, crept downstairs carefully avoiding the third step from the bottom.

He opened the kitchen curtains but it was still too dark for him to see the food dish, so he switched on the outside light by the back door. He peered at the dish through the window. It was empty, all the food had gone!

Wow, Lucky must have been very hungry, he thought. A

plan began forming in his mind. Tonight, he would creep downstairs during the night and keep a lookout for her. Obviously, he couldn't tell his mum and David what he planned to do. They would never allow him to do it. He switched off the light and began to creep back to his bedroom.

"William is that you?" his mother whispered from her bedroom.

William froze on the spot. "Yes Mum," William whispered, "I was just checking the food bowl to see if Lucky had been."

"Just you hurry up back to bed and mind you don't wake David."

"Okay, sorry I woke you Mum," whispered William.

Later that morning, as William was fastening up his coat getting ready for school, he was relieved that his mum had not said anything about him waking her up earlier.

"Cheerio Mum," he said, as he turned to give her a hug.

"Now be a good boy, work hard and have a nice day," she replied.

At school, nothing unusual happened during the morning. After lunch break, Mrs Jackson explained to the class that they would be doing Art and Craft to create a backdrop for the Guy Fawkes display in the main corridor. Mrs Jackson cleared her throat, something she always did before speaking to the whole class.

"Uh hmm, listen up Class 6. As you know, you can

work with whomever you want during Art and Craft lessons, on one condition," she paused scanning the class, "and what is that one condition Tommy?"

"As long as we work together nicely, Mrs Jackson," he replied.

"Well done Tommy, that is correct. Now quickly decide who you are going to work with."

Immediately, chairs scraped and children stood up, signalling to one another as they joined their friends. William and Jason, as usual, were the odd ones out. Nobody signalled to them. It was always the same, even when some children were absent, and there were spare places at some of the tables.

Jason sat quietly in his wheelchair; he'd been born with a problem with his back which meant he'd been unable to walk without leg braces and crutches. Miss Frederick, the classroom assistant, helped him to get around the school.

William really liked Jason and thought he was very brave but he really would like to make some new friends. He had tried to make friends by working harder, and impressing his classmates, but it had gone badly wrong for him. Whenever he got a 'merit' star for maths from Mrs Jackson, some of the boys called him names such as 'Lippy Swot' or 'The Freaky Geek'…

William's mind went back to the first day after the summer holidays, when Mrs Jackson had called out William's new surname, Harrison, as she had taken the register. Tommy Smithers had heard that William's new stepdad was Mr Harrison, the deputy head at the comprehensive school that his older brother went to.

Later, at morning break, Tommy had spied the opportunity to tease William. He'd waited in the playground with a group of his friends and, as William wandered across the yard, he had called out, "Hey you! Billy Harrison, are you a new kid?"

William ignored the taunt at first but other children started laughing. Tommy was smirking now as he continued, "I thought your name was Billy Boffin."

William sensed he was blushing and his hands were bunching into fists inside his coat pockets. Tommy started chanting, "Bill-y Boff-in, Bill-y Boff-in," and pointing at William. The other children again joined in, "Bill-y Boff-in, Bill-y Boff-in," they chanted, and they too started jabbing their fingers at William. It had been horrible and William had felt a burning rage building inside him. He hated Tommy, and at that moment he really wanted to punch him in the face, to shut him up.

He was just about to go and punch him when a voice in his head said, *'Don't do it, you'll only get into trouble. Your mum will be really upset again. Walk away and calm down William.'* So, instead of fighting Tommy, he turned and ran back into the school and hid in the boys' toilets.

As the bell rang signalling the end of playtime, Mrs Jackson saw him coming out of the toilets and asked, "Are you feeling okay William? You look a bit upset."

"I'm fine miss," he replied, just as Tommy entered the room. As he walked behind Mrs Jackson he stared straight at William and stuck his tongue out. William decided not to say anything about the name-calling to Mrs Jackson, because he was sure that it would only make things worse…

Recently, just before the half-term break, Tommy had been involved in another cruel and spiteful incident. He had called Jason a 'zombie', and then proceeded to copy the way he walked on his crutches. Some of the boys thought it was funny and began copying Tommy. William was really upset for Jason and he felt his temper boiling up again! Except this time, it was just too much and he charged into Tommy, knocking him over and they had started fighting. Despite Jason explaining why William had attacked Tommy, the incident had caused William to get into a lot of trouble with both Mrs Hargreaves, the head teacher, and at home. Mrs Hargreaves decided that because William had started the fight, he had to say sorry to Tommy for knocking him over. Also he had to promise not to get involved in fighting in the future. Mrs Hargreaves had also given Tommy a telling-off and he had to apologise to Jason and promise never to taunt him again.

William was unable to concentrate on painting the backdrop of the Houses of Parliament. However, his daydreaming was ended when Mrs Jackson cleared her throat and told the class to hang their work on the drying racks and clean up their brushes. Moments later the bell rang signalling home time.

Within seconds of Mrs Jackson dismissing the class, William had grabbed his coat and began racing home.

It would probably have been quicker on the bus, but he couldn't stand the idea of being taunted and laughed at by Colin and Johnno Taylor. Just as he hoped, there was nobody at home. His mum wouldn't normally be home for at least another half an hour. The light was already starting to fade and he was desperate to go and search for Lucky before it was too dark.

He raced upstairs and quickly changed out of his school uniform, scrambled into his jeans and pulled on his blue jumper. He reached for the torch out of the kitchen cupboard and stuffed it in his pocket. Then he grabbed his coat and scarf before putting on his wellingtons. He remembered that the grass was wet in the orchard and he was planning to search the hedgerows. He realised that it was going to be very difficult to find Lucky, but he desperately wanted to see his friend again.

He was just reaching out to open the front door when he heard the key turn in the lock. *It must be his mum! Oh no, she was home early!*

"Hello son, where are you off to at this time?" she asked, surprised to see William already changed and about to go out, "it will be dark soon."

He didn't know why he said it, it just came straight out of his mouth. "Oh I'm just going to meet a friend, no one you know, I won't be long."

He hoped that would be the end of the conversation

but his mum seemed pleased and wanted to know more.

"Oh, that's nice, is it someone from school? What's their name?"

"Yes," he lied, "just someone from school." William had never lied to his mum before, but he decided that if he'd told her the truth about going to try and find Lucky, she would probably stop him from going.

"Well, okay, but don't be long. I'm putting tea on the table at six; it's pizza tonight, your favourite, and you know David will not be happy if you are not here when it's ready."

William would never forget how angry David had been with him when he'd not come down for his tea after his mum had called him to come to the table. He had been playing 'Zoo Keeper' on his computer and he needed to get a vet to treat his prized bull elephant or it would die. He daren't stop or he would have been timed out. Eventually, when he did come down the stairs, there was no meal in his place.

David had shouted at him, saying that if he couldn't be bothered to come for his meal, he could do without it. Not only that, but to teach William a lesson, he'd removed William's computer from his room.

Eventually, he was allowed to eat his meal, after he'd said how truly sorry he was to his mum. Even then, he'd spotted his mum giving David one of those looks that adults do to each other all the time. Later that evening, as David was removing his computer, he reminded William never to be late for meals again.

Despite his repeated apologies and promising never to be late for a meal again, it still took David three days before he agreed that William could have his computer back. William also had to do the washing-up for the rest of the week.

William didn't want to go through all that again, so this time he just said quickly, "Okay Mum, love you, bye!" and with that he dashed out and began running down the path towards the gate into the orchard.

Chapter 10

The Plan Goes Wrong

Late afternoon, Wednesday November 1st

William looked around, but quickly realised that his plan was almost certainly doomed to failure. He had no idea where to start looking for Lucky. A little hedgehog could be anywhere. He even tried squatting down and listening, just in case he could make out any rustling sounds, but gave that up straight away. It was hopeless.

In the gathering gloom, the branches of the trees appeared dark and menacing and suddenly a shiver ran down his spine.

'Whoo hoo hoo,' called the owl from a tree close by and William nearly jumped out of his skin. William began feeling really scared now. Turning around, he dashed back towards the house as fast as he could. As he ran, the torch swung wildly, its beam briefly lighting up everything it touched with a pale, ghostly glow.

When he reached the house he was puffing hard and he leant against the wall, waiting to get his breath back. Then he remembered seeing some workmen in the park over the road. They had been cutting the branches off some of the trees and leaving them in piles. He'd read on the internet that hedgehogs often make their winter dens in piles of branches and leaves, so it might be worth a look. He switched off the torch in case his mum spotted the beam through the window and called him in.

Walking on tiptoe, he crept past the back door and at the end of the drive he turned to walk along the pavement by the road. There was a hole in the grass verge where some workmen had been digging. Above it was a red and white warning sign propped against some stakes to stop anyone falling in. He shone his torch into the hole in case Lucky had fallen in. No sign of Lucky there.

As he got to the corner, a car came around the bend, its headlights revealing a lump on the road. Before he could identify what it was, the headlights dazzled him. The car sped past on its way. The street lamp did not provide enough light for William to be able to see clearly what the lump on the road was. So, checking carefully to see if there were any more cars coming, he stepped out into the road shining his torch on the lump. He saw immediately that it was some poor, unfortunate animal that had been run over. As he got closer he could see exactly what it was… it was a hedgehog!

"Oh no, not you Lucky!" He couldn't bear it if Lucky had been run over, so soon after he'd set her free. He crouched down for a better look at the hapless creature. His eyes prickled with tears as he shone the torch onto the animal. He could see that much of its body had been crushed. The spines on its back were flattened and bits of its guts spilled out onto the tarmac. The hedgehog's head remained unmarked; it looked really big against its flattened body. Gingerly he lifted the head for a better look and then he shone the torch on the poor creature's jaw… it was perfectly straight.

"Phew, thank goodness," he mumbled, as relief washed over him. It couldn't be Lucky. This was a different hedgehog. He gently lowered the head back onto the road.

Suddenly, he was lit up by the dazzling headlights of an oncoming car rushing towards him. He could see the red bonnet hurtling in his direction. It was so close he could see the separate headlights clearly and glimpsed the dark shape of the driver behind the steering wheel. The car tyres squealed as the driver braked and swerved trying to avoid smashing into him. The car horn blared twice as William leapt for his life, landing heavily in the gutter. He felt the wind from the speeding car rush past him as it sped by, its red brake lights blinking, as the driver wrestled with the wheel to avoid skidding into the ditch.

William instantly jumped to his feet and ran across the road into the park and hid behind the hedge. He watched in horror as he saw the car stop and begin turning around. The driver was obviously really mad at him and was going to come after him.

Moments later, the car screeched to a stop opposite the park entrance and the driver got out and called out, "Hello, William is that you?" There was a moment's silence before the driver called again, "William, where are you? Are you injured?" There was another pause as the man waited for a reply. William was too frightened to answer, even though he recognised the voice.

"Come on William, I could have killed you. I just need to know that you're not hurt."

He crouched down even lower onto the wet grass and held his breath. The man paced up and down for a few moments before getting back into his car, reversing into the park entrance and continuing on his way.

William gave a huge sigh of relief. '*That was lucky, I could've been killed,*' he thought as he brushed his hands against his coat trying to clean off the worst of the dirt. In the glow from the street light he could see that his coat was smeared with dirt and the palms of his hands were scratched and stinging with grit.

"Oh no, Mum will kill me when she sees the mess I've made of my coat," he mumbled to himself. He couldn't see the torch anywhere, but as he crossed the road there it was on the tarmac… it was crushed flat.

Chapter 11

I Need To Find A New Den

At the same time, Wednesday November 1st

Following my battle with that brute I was feeling very sore. I spent my first night back in the wild sleeping under some dry leaves that had been blown into a heap against the fence. It was already quite dark when I woke up. I yawned and stretched out, uncurling myself slowly. I felt really stiff, my muscles ached and when I took a deep breath a sharp pain stabbed my side. My injured jaw was throbbing, reminding me not to get into any more fights. Next time I might not be so lucky.

I sniffed the night air to see if there were any strange new smells around. A strange smell could mean more danger, so I checked first, just as my mother had taught us when we were tiny 'hoglets'. I strained my ears, to listen carefully too. The breeze was rustling some dry leaves. I could hear a moth flittering around the bushes to my right and a dog was yapping excitedly in the distance. There appeared to be nothing too unusual or suspicious so I cautiously poked my nose out through the leaves and blinked my eyes. I waited as my eyes adjusted to the bright moonlight and shapes and shadows started to become clearer.

I could just make out a path to a house with a vegetable patch on the right. There was an old shed in the corner behind some fruit bushes with their thin reedy stems, and the slim trunks of two fruit trees to my left.

I had checked out the shed last night to see if it might make a good place for my 'big sleep'. There was a really strong odour coming from underneath it; it was a smell that I didn't recognise.

Particularly after my encounter with that brute, I decided not to risk it. I needed to find a safe, new den and quickly, but first I needed to eat. I couldn't see any threat, so I moved forward cautiously, my nerves tingling, expecting some new danger at any moment. I could hear one of those machines roaring down the road...

Suddenly, 'BLEEEEEP, BLEEEEEP' a dreadful sound shattered the quiet of the evening. I stopped, not daring to make a sound. *'What was that?'* I wondered, *'could it be another monster? Was the creature out hunting?'* Anxiously, I waited in the shadows of the fruit bushes, my heart pounding and my ears straining.

I remained absolutely still, and I could hear

someone calling out several times. After a few moments I heard a machine roaring off and quietness returned, except for my gurgling tummy which was telling me that I was hungry, as if I didn't know.

I began searching for a tasty meal. Within minutes I came across an unwary young slug under some leaves and then another really squishy one.

'Well that's a good start,' I told myself, 'but I would really like some nice wriggly worms.' I made my way towards the vegetable patch and sniffed at the pile of canes by the fence.

'*There's a good chance of a tasty beetle or two in there,*' I thought, and so, using my front feet, I rolled some canes out of the way and began sniffing in between the gaps. Sure enough, there was a large beetle tucking into some white ant eggs. '*Perfect,*' I thought, as I made short work of it, crunching its hard shell with my needle-sharp teeth. There were some small, juicy snails sticking to the cane and I finished them off too in double-quick time.

By now the moon was very bright and it was starting to feel really chilly.

'*I must find a nice warm den for my big sleep, the frosts are on the way,*' I thought to myself. However, I knew that I needed to keep eating to build myself up to survive the cold winter months when there is little food about.

Fortunately, a big, slimy, black slug was slowly slithering its way towards the rows of cabbages and sprouts. I waited in the shadows as its long body slid slowly towards me. Then, making a quick check to make sure that there was nothing else around, I made my move. My front claws gripped the soft fleshy body whilst my sharp teeth did the rest. This particularly gooey treat was a great way to finish my evening feed. Feeling very pleased with myself, and with a full tummy, I now felt like a drink to wash down all that food. I noticed several small puddles in between the rows of cabbages.

As I looked into the still water, I could see the reflection of the moon in the clear sky. It had a light blue ring around it. I remember our mother telling us that if the 'Great Hedgehog' who watches over everything was wearing a blue collar we must get ready for the 'big sleep.' I began to lap up the water and I was surprised how icy cold it tasted. In fact, there was a thin skin of ice forming at the edges of the puddle. I made my way back to the pile of leaves against the fence panel before burrowing my way under the leaves and curling up really tightly. I made my mind up that tomorrow, I really would have to find a nice warm den for my big sleep...

Chapter 12

Imaginary Friends To The Rescue

Tea-time, Wednesday November 1st

Just as Lucky was tucking into the slug, William was kicking off his wellington boots having made his way back home. He'd checked to see if David's car was on the driveway. Pleased that it wasn't, he opened the back door as quietly as he could. He was hoping to sneak upstairs without his mum seeing him or the dirt on his coat.

"Is that you William?" his mum called from the kitchen, "You're just in time, David's called to say that's he's running a little late, so I've not put the pizza in yet." Just then she turned around catching William trying to tiptoe his way up to his bedroom.

"Goodness William, whatever happened to you?

Are you hurt? Have you been in a fight? Did those boys pick on you again? We need to get David to find them and sort this out, I bet they go to his school," she gabbled without pausing for breath.

William spotted his chance to keep out of trouble, "I'm not hurt Mum. They chased after me in the park and I tripped as I was running away." As soon as he spoke he realised that he was lying again. That was the second time in one night. Telling lies was becoming a habit... a very bad habit.

He looked down and continued, "I'm sorry about messing up my coat and I think the torch dropped out of my pocket when I fell."

"Don't worry about the coat, slip it off and I'll put it in the wash so that it can dry overnight." Then she noticed the scratches on his hands. "Oh William, just look at your hands, we need to get them washed so that we can clean up those grazes straight away."

For the next few minutes William's mum took charge, fussing around, running a sink of hot water and getting disinfectant from the bathroom cabinet. The water turned a milky colour and she began gently sponging his hands and removing the grit.

"You'd better put those trousers in the wash too, there's dirt on the knees."

William couldn't believe how well his lie had worked. It would certainly have been a different story if David had been home. Whenever William was in trouble his mum always found a way to make him feel better, whereas David usually told him off and sent him to his room.

William remembered the time when his real dad was alive and he'd knocked over a glass vase. It had broken and he had bent down to pick up the shattered glass. His Dad had quickly picked him up and checked he hadn't cut himself and didn't get angry with him at all. In fact, William couldn't remember his real dad ever being cross or shouting at him or his mum... ever.

During the move to this new house, William had been really upset when his mum had packed away all the photographs of his real dad. William had sneaked one into his school bag and later he'd hidden it in the desk drawer in his bedroom...

"You dry yourself off and get changed ready for tea and I'll make us both a hot chocolate, how's that?" his mum said, smiling as she ran her fingers through his hair.

"Great Mum, and thanks for not being mad about the coat."

William went up to his bedroom and took the photo from the desk drawer. The photo showed his real dad holding him by the hand; it had been taken years ago when they were visiting his grandparents.

"Dad, I'm really sorry that I lied to Mum, I just wanted to see Lucky again. I promise I won't lie to her again."

He put on some jeans and the thick pullover his gran had given him for his birthday. It had a picture of a cartoon lion on the front and William remembered thinking it was much too babyish for him. His mum had said, "How lovely, put it on." When he saw himself in the mirror he had decided never to wear it again, especially when he was out, just in case anyone from school saw him. It definitely was 'not cool', and it was too small anyway. Of course, William was too polite to say anything. He had thanked his gran and had given her a kiss on the cheek. He'd hated that part, her skin felt rough and she had long bristles sprouting out of a wart on her chin. William thought it was just like a witch in the fairy stories he'd read when he was younger. Once when he'd asked his mum about it, she'd told him not to mention it ever again, it would be rude. She added that it was like his lip, after a while nobody noticed it. His mum called up from the kitchen, "Your drink's ready, don't let it go cold."

"Thanks Mum, on my way."

Downstairs he settled onto the kitchen stool and reached for his mug. The sweet smell of the frothy chocolate made him feel warm inside. His mum noticed the pullover and said, "That's nice, your gran will be pleased you like it."

"It's lovely," William replied, meaning the chocolate not the pullover, so he didn't think it counted as a lie this time.

Chapter 13

More Lies

Tea-time, Wednesday November 1st

Just then, the sound of the car pulling up on the drive interrupted their conversation. William heard the engine stop, followed by the familiar footsteps on the path before the keys rattled in the lock and the door opened.

'*What if his mum says something?*' William's mind was racing, '*David would get to the truth and then he'd be really mad with him.*' William felt his hands go sweaty and his heart started thumping.

"Hi, I'm sorry I'm late, gosh it's freezing out there," David said, as he put his large briefcase down. "I hope you've saved me some pizza." He smiled when he noticed William's pullover. "Nice one," he said as he tousled William's hair. William hated it whenever he did that. Then David moved across the kitchen to kiss Margaret. It was one of those pecks on the cheek kisses, not like you see people do in films, when they are supposed to really love each other. William often wondered if his mum and David really loved each other as he'd never seen them kissing like that.

Mind you, on second thoughts, William decided, it would be too gross to see them having a full-on snog like they do in films.

"We waited for you love. I'll put the pizza in now. Why don't you go and change out of your suit?" William's mum suggested.

"Good plan," replied David, and he went upstairs. William took another sip of his chocolate and began to relax. He was pretty sure now that his mum wasn't going to say anything about the coat or the boys chasing him.

Just then the telephones began ringing in the hallway and his parents' bedroom. David called down, "I've got it," and the ringing stopped. William took no notice at first until he heard David say, "Are you sure it was William? He's in the kitchen, but he looks fine to me and we're about to have our tea." Suddenly, William was straining to hear every word.

"Sounds like he was extremely lucky," David said, before continuing, "Are you okay? You must be pretty shaken up...."

There was a pause as the caller must have been talking.

"It's really kind of you to check that he's not

hurt." There was another long pause before David continued, "Yes, yes, of course, I'll speak to him and make sure he knows not to be so stupid again. Are you sure you still want him to come on Saturday morning?"

William had recognised Mr Wilson's voice when he'd called out and now he realised that it must be him on the phone. There was a long silence as Mr Wilson was obviously speaking again. William sipped his chocolate, anxiously dreading what would happen when David came downstairs.

David began speaking again. "About ten o'clock then. I am really sorry about the fright he caused you tonight. Thanks again for being so understanding; we'll see you on Saturday morning then, bye."

The call ended and William waited for the terrible storm that he felt sure was building upstairs, certain that it was about to unleash itself on him. For the third time that night he felt very scared.

Soon, David came downstairs and returned to the kitchen wearing jeans and a green pullover. William's mum was checking the oven to see if the pizza was ready. William avoided looking at David; instead he studied the frothy bubbles on the top of his hot chocolate.

"William, could you get the knives, forks and trays please? We'll eat it in front of the telly," she asked before adding, "Who was that on the phone?"

David replied, "Oh, it was Mr Wilson, you know, the vet."

"Oh, what did he want? Was he ringing about

William going to the Rescue Centre on Saturday? He can still go can't he?" she asked anxiously.

"Blimey Margaret, one question a time. Yes, William can go, Mr Wilson would like him there at ten o'clock, and he'll need to wear jeans and wellingtons as he is going to be helping his wife who runs the Rescue Centre."

"That's great news, isn't it son?" she said smiling at William.

William didn't trust himself to reply so he busied himself in the cutlery drawer, still avoiding looking at David and he simply mumbled, "Yes that's great," waiting for his lies to be exposed and the telling-off that was bound to follow.

Chapter 14

Suspected Of Telling Lies

Tea-time, Wednesday November 1st (continued)

"Now then young man, is there something you'd like to tell us, something that happened this evening?" His stepdad was peering at him over his spectacles. He was looking straight into William's eyes, which is exactly what detectives, teachers and some fathers do whenever they are checking to see if you are telling lies. David often told them about how clever he'd been working out who the culprits were when an incident happened at school. He was good at getting to the truth.

As William weighed up his reply, his mum suddenly came to the rescue, at least for a moment.

"Come on, let's eat, this pizza will go cold," she said.

William picked up a slice and took a big bite and began chewing slowly, hoping this would buy him some time whilst he thought about what to say. He knew that he would be in serious trouble if he admitted that he'd almost been killed by Mr Wilson because he was looking at a dead hedgehog in the middle of the road. It would mean admitting to his mum that he'd lied to her about meeting a friend and also being chased by the boys.

"This is terrific, Mum," he said, but before he could take another bite David said, "Where are your manners William? You might eat like that in the street, but in this house we use a knife and fork."

"Sorry," he mumbled, picking up his knife and fork.

"Well, we're still waiting young man. What happened this evening?" David said impatiently.

William decided to stick to his story about the boys chasing him and that he'd tripped over a log as he was fleeing from them, to avoid getting a 'beating' from them.

"Were they the same boys who were stealing our apples when you saved Lucky?" asked his mum, before turning to David adding, "They probably go to your school, David. Surely there must be a way of finding out who they are."

"Of course I can, once William here gives me a good description. It could be anybody," he replied sharply. There was definitely an edge to his voice now.

"Did you get a good look at them?" he asked.

"No, It was dark; they just started running after me, so I didn't see them clearly," William lied again.

"Let's start from the beginning then shall we? How many boys were there?"

William hesitated before replying, "Three I think."

"Some of the staff might know their names if we know which year group they are in," his stepdad suggested, before continuing, "How big were they compared to you? Stand up, show me."

William realised that David was in full detective mode now. He was going to try and solve this imaginary crime. William stood up and held his right hand up a few centimetres above his head. "They were about this big," he said, moving his hand up and down a few centimetres, being deliberately vague.

"Were they all about that height? Were any of them bigger or smaller?" probed his stepdad.

Sitting back down, William took another mouthful of pizza, shrugged his shoulders, before explaining that he couldn't be sure because he didn't hang about to find out.

"You're not giving me much to go on are you, son?" David said, his voice clearly suggesting that he knew William was not telling the truth.

David turned again and looked straight into William's eyes. His voice was getting more menacing as he spoke. "Okay, we're not getting anywhere are we? Can you explain to me why Mr Wilson rang to make sure you weren't injured after he nearly killed you in his car? What on earth were you playing at lad?"

"Oh no!" his mum gasped.

William gulped hard, his mind scrambling to find a suitable answer. "I dashed across the road and tripped over just as the car was coming round the bend. I'm sorry I didn't tell you but I didn't want to worry you, Mum."

"Oh, good heavens William, that explains why your hands were scratched," his mum said soothingly as she got up from her chair to embrace him in a hug.

"I'm really sorry about the torch Mum," William mumbled as he snuggled up into her arms.

"Well, no harm's done, eh David, now let's finish off this pizza before it gets cold. Now who's for more salad?" she asked cheerily, putting another slice of pizza on William's plate.

David did ask him a couple more questions about the imaginary attackers, but thankfully his mum gave David a look which suggested 'that's enough', and he let it go. William finished off his pizza, relieved that his mum appeared to have forgotten about his meeting with his imaginary new friend. He smiled to himself as he realised how useful all these imaginary people had turned out to be.

"I'm feeling a bit tired now," William said. "I think I'll just put some food out for Lucky, in case she's hungry, and go to bed…"

He got up and gave them both a good night hug.

"It'll be the shock, love," said his mum. "Don't worry, you'll be fine after a good night's sleep."

David held William by the shoulders and looked into his eyes as he said, "Good night young man, if you can give me something to go on, I'll find out who those boys are, that's a promise."

William went into the kitchen and took down the chicken-flavoured cat food. He opened the can and forked some into the same bowl he'd used the night before. William thought it looked like lumpy sick but Lucky had gobbled it up the night before so he felt certain she would come back for some more. He went outside and placed the bowl carefully this time so he would be able to see it using the light from the garage. The switch was by the door although it didn't give off as much light as the passage light over the door, but his parents were less likely to notice if he switched that on during the night. As he squatted down by the bowl he began to speak quietly:

"Lucky, wherever you are, I hope you are finding enough to eat and are keeping warm. This is for you; please come and see me, I miss you. Good night Lucky."

He made his way back through the kitchen calling out a final "good night" and began to go up the stairs. Once again he carefully placed his clothes so that he would be able to get dressed in the dark. He paid particular attention to placing his slippers under the bed where he could reach them easily. The plan was set. He daren't set his alarm clock or the alarm on his mobile as they would wake his parents up. As he saw it he had no choice; he would just have to pretend to be asleep and stay awake all night!

Chapter 15

William Tries Another Plan

Before dawn, Thursday November 2nd

Despite his efforts to stay awake, William must have fallen asleep. He woke up suddenly. He wondered what time it was as it was still dark outside. He lay still, listening carefully. The house was so quiet that he could even make out the regular tick-tock of the clock on the mantelpiece in the lounge. Just then, it made a slight whirring sound, which William knew happened just before it chimed. He counted the chimes on his fingers. One, two, three, four, and then it stopped. It must be four o'clock in the morning. He rubbed the sleep from his eyes and stretched his arms up above his head and yawned.

Without turning on the light, he waited until his eyes became more used to the darkness. He fumbled for his slippers before putting them on. He pulled on his pullover as the room felt cold. Then, stepping lightly on tiptoe, he made his way round his bed to the door. He'd left it slightly open so that it wouldn't wake his parents but now it was closed. '*How could that be?*' he pondered briefly before realising that it must have been his mum when she checked to see if he was asleep. She must have closed the door.

The door opened with a sharp click and William listened, not daring to breathe, before stepping out onto the landing. The night light cast its dim, yellow glow making the photos of Nan and Grandad appear very scary. They appeared to be watching him. Grandad was looking quite severe, as if he was about to tell him off for telling lies, whilst Nan had a smile touching the edge of her lips, as if she understood why he'd made up the story about the boys. The only sound coming from his parents' room was the noise of David's loud snoring. He wanted to laugh as he sounded like a pig but he managed to stop himself.

'*That's good,*' he thought, and then slowly, step by step, he tiptoed along the landing, taking care not to step on any of the creaky floorboards. As he proceeded down the stairs, he paused, careful to avoid those steps that creaked.

He gripped hold of the banister as he tried to step over the third step from the bottom but his slipper started to come off. His foot landed heavily with a dull thump. He remained absolutely still, not moving a muscle; his heart was pounding as he waited for any movement coming from his mum's bedroom. He expected David to come rushing out at any moment. He dared not move, and his eyes picked out the dark shadows of the sofa and fireplace. The only sound was the ticking of the clock.

Once he was sure that nobody had woken up, he made his way towards the kitchen door. He turned the handle very hesitantly and winced when it made a loud click. Thankfully, the hinges didn't squeak as he stepped into the kitchen. He walked increasingly confidently towards the outside door and switched on the garage light. A pool of yellow light flooded the side passage. William stared at the bowl and it certainly looked empty. Unfortunately he couldn't be sure because the side of the bowl cast a shadow across it. William scanned around for any sign of Lucky…

Suddenly, everything became incredibly bright as the lights came on. The harsh light made William blink and he raised his arm to block out the sudden glare. David was standing right behind him in his pyjamas; he was holding his cricket bat in one hand, his hair was untidy and his face was flushed bright red.

"It's you… you idiot!" scolded David. "What do you think you're doing down here at this time of night?" Then, turning to look upstairs, he called, "It's only William, Margaret." Turning back to William he whispered through gritted teeth, "You nearly gave me a heart attack. Your mum was sure that there were burglars in the house."

"I'm really sorry," William said. "I just wanted to see if the food had gone."

David whispered again through gritted teeth, "You and that flipping hedgehog are nothing but trouble!"

Moments later William's mum entered the kitchen, wearing her nightdress and dressing gown. "What's that about the food's gone? What are you doing down here son? Is everything all right William?"

"Yes, we're all fine and we've seen off the intruders, eh lad," joked David. "Let's put the kettle on; we may as well as we are all up now anyway."

William couldn't quite believe that David had not carried on shouting at him in front of his mum; instead he had included him in the joke.

"Good idea," said his mum. "Goodness William, you gave me a fright when I heard someone on the stairs. Anyway, let's take our drinks back to bed and try and get some sleep, after all it's still the middle of the night!"

William sat up in bed cradling his mug in both hands, sipping the sweet chocolate. *At least I know Lucky is not far away, even if she is hungry*, he thought to himself. He finished his drink and snuggled down into a deep sleep.

Just two gardens away I was also awake. I'd been fast asleep in my bed of leaves when I'd been woken up by the noise of tin cans and bottles clattering onto a

69

path. I peeked out between the leaves of my den and watched, staying absolutely still. I waited anxiously in case it was the monster hunting for food. A few moments later, the culprit appeared. *It was a fox!* I recognised it from the tales our mum had told us. I did not move a muscle as it came trotting down the garden. The frost-covered lawn twinkled in the moonlight like the stars on a clear night. I could see it had something in its mouth. The fox paused to look around before stooping low and disappearing under the shed. So now I know what that awful smell is, it is Mr Fox, and he's not going hungry tonight either. I shuffled back into my bed of leaves and snuggled down again back into a deep sleep.

Chapter 16

A Day To Remember

Morning, Thursday November 2nd

William was sound asleep when his mum called him to get ready for school. He felt very tired with thoughts swirling around in his mind. He wondered why David had not gone barmy at him. Instead he'd included him in his joke with his mum. It was not like him at all.

He placed his hands behind his head thinking about school and the day ahead. This week at school, the class had been working on the story of Guy Fawkes and the 'Gunpowder Plot' to blow up the Houses of Parliament. When William told David, he had joked that things might have turned out better if they had succeeded!

His mum had chuckled at first before saying, "Don't say such a thing, David, especially not in front of William; he'll think you approve of violence."

"He knows I was only kidding," he said, leaning across and tousling William's hair with his right hand. "It was exactly like those terrorists on the news who blow things up. Guy Fawkes and the other plotters were prepared to fight others to try and make a point."

William must have drifted off back to sleep because the next thing he knew his mum was shouting him to get up. "William, come on son, your clean shirt is hanging in the wardrobe, and don't forget to have a good wash."

"Okay Mum, I'm moving."

"I'll move you if you don't get a shift on. Do you want a lift or don't you?" called David in that sharp voice of his.

Chapter 11

The New Girl

Morning, Thursday November 2nd

It began like any other school day in Class 6. William was sitting at his usual table in class. The other tables had four or five pupils sitting around them as Mrs Jackson called the register. The only other person at William's table was Jason. Janet occasionally sat at their table but she was away again. William was not surprised as she hardly ever attended school. When she did, her clothes were often filthy and she looked like she hadn't had a bath in ages. Once, she smelled so badly that some of the pupils were really horrid, calling her names and making her cry.

William remembered that the nurse had taken her out of the class to talk to her. William didn't think it was fair to put Jason, Janet and himself on the same table. "It just makes us stand out more, so the others can pick on us," he'd complained to his mum.

Just then, there was a knock on the door and when it opened Mrs Hargreaves, the head teacher, was standing there with a new pupil.

"Good morning Class 6, and good morning to you, Mrs Jackson."

The class chanted their reply emphasising every syllable:

"Good mor-ning Mrs Har-greaves."

"Thank you Class 6. Now, may I introduce Parveen; she is joining your class from today. I'm sure that you will all do your best to make her feel very welcome and help her to settle in."

Mrs Jackson stood up. "Good morning Parveen, it's lovely to have you in our class." She walked towards William's table and pulled out a chair. "Now then, why don't you come and sit over here at this table with William and Jason. I'm sure they will make you feel welcome."

William could hear the sniggers of some of the boys and he caught Thelma Wilks pulling a face as if she had a plate of live worms placed in front of her for dinner. Whilst Mrs Jackson fussed around getting some exercise books for the new girl, Jason leaned across and introduced himself. "Hello Parveen, I'm Jason," and William added quickly, "and I'm William."

Mrs Jackson cleared her throat, as usual, before speaking to the whole class.

"Uh hmm, Class 6, this morning we are going to do some more work on decimals. Then, after break, you are going to imagine you are newspaper reporters and the big story is the arrest of Guy Fawkes for trying to blow up the Houses of Parliament." She then quickly explained what each of the different groups was to do. She asked the classroom assistant, Miss Faulkner, to help the blue group get started and finally said that she wanted to spend a few minutes with Parveen.

For the next hour, each of the groups was busy, working hard on their maths. Little was said on William's table, but whenever he looked up Parveen was sucking on her pen, concentrating hard on her maths. He noticed that her long black hair was very clean and shiny. Parveen glanced towards William and smiled.

Clearing her throat, Mrs Jackson announced that she wanted everyone's books passed to the front table as she was going to mark them. The bell sounded and she dismissed the class, one table at a time. She asked Katie Waterstone to show Parveen where the toilets were and how she could get a drink, or a piece of toast from the dining hall. Katie was a popular girl, who had lots of friends, so William thought that Mrs Jackson had made a good choice.

Later in the playground he noticed that Katie and Parveen were surrounded by pupils and Parveen was looking upset, as if she was trying not to cry.

William overheard Tommy Smithers say loudly, "Don't touch her Katie; you'll catch something 'orrible."

William ran to find Mrs Hudson, the playground supervisor, and tell her that Tommy was being cruel again. Unfortunately he couldn't find her. So he ran back to his classroom and burst into the room. Mrs Jackson was at her desk marking the maths books,

"Goodness me, William, that's no way to enter a classroom. Is there a fire?"

"No Mrs Jackson, you'll have to come quickly, Tommy Smithers is saying horrible things about Parveen and she's getting upset. I couldn't find Mrs Hudson so I came to find you."

"Well, we can't have that, can we? Now let's go and get this nonsense stopped."

With that she got up from her seat and marched out, William hurried to keep up with her as she strode out into the playground. She cleared her throat and immediately the crowd started to move away.

"What's going on here then?" she demanded, her eyes scanning for pupils that she thought would be prepared to speak up.

"Nothing Mrs Jackson, we were just talking to Parveen," said Tommy's friend, Colin.

Many of the pupils moved further away and those who remained were now looking down at their feet. Everybody was avoiding making eye contact with Mrs Jackson.

"Is that how it was Katie?" asked Mrs Jackson.

Katie looked around and saw the look on the boys' faces warning her not to 'grass' on them and so she said, "Yes, Mrs Jackson." She paused, as if thinking, and then said, "They were just asking Parveen where she'd come from."

Before Mrs Jackson could continue, the bell rang and the pupils raced to form straight lines by the door nearest to their classroom.

Class 6 were soon ready, and she invited them to follow her down the corridor and into their room. As William was hanging his coat on his peg, he felt a hard shove in the back which caused him to stagger. He heard some boys laugh, and as he turned around he was faced by Tommy Smithers, who whispered menacingly, "I'll get you for that, Lippy, you '*grasser*', just you wait."

Back in the classroom, Parveen was still looking upset, and as William sat down he thought she had been very brave not to cry. Mrs Jackson seemed to have forgotten all about the incident as she began explaining the next activity to the class. Pointing at the whiteboard she said:

"Now, I've written the key objectives on the whiteboard here. I want you to imagine you are journalists who are reporting on the biggest story of the century. You will need to use the computers and the resource books at the back of the room to research what happened. Remember to use the 'success criteria' for newspaper reports that I taught you. I want each group to draft a report."

She paused before she continued, "William and Jason, can you work with Parveen please? You will need to explain the key points of the 'Gunpowder Plot' to her."

William soon forgot about Tommy Smithers and for the rest of the morning he worked with Parveen and Jason on their newspaper report. For once he really enjoyed himself. He discovered that Parveen's second name was Bedi. He learned that her family had moved from Fordingley to take over the post office and shop in the village. She had an older brother called Manjit, who was studying at Manchester University, and an older sister, Narinder, who went to the comprehensive in Camford. William explained to Parveen that his stepdad was the deputy head of that school, so he would probably know her.

Jason was particularly good at spelling, but his handwriting was even more spidery than William's, so Parveen volunteered to write down their ideas and William felt quite jealous as her writing was very neat and easy to read, unlike his scrawl. She hesitated when she was not sure how to spell a particular word or name, but Jason soon helped out. Whenever they needed some more information, William went to the computer to do some research.

As he was returning to their table, he saw Tommy re-enter the class after visiting the toilet. Tommy was smiling, as if he was pleased with himself about something, and he jabbed his finger towards William with a smirk. Back in his place, William glanced towards Tommy's table and saw that Colin and Johnno were both grinning at him. William had an uneasy feeling that something was wrong. At least the new information he'd found out helped their report take shape.

"We need some pictures of Guy Fawkes," suggested Jason, so when one of the computers became free they all gathered around it. William positioned Jason, in his wheelchair, directly in front of the screen. Within minutes, they had a selection of images of Guy Fawkes from cartoons to old paintings. Parveen picked out a portrait of Guy that looked the most like a photograph and the two boys agreed they should use it. Jason then suggested that they include a picture of the Houses of Parliament and yet again they were spoilt for choice.

Suddenly, Mrs Jackson cleared her throat, "Uh hmm, listen everyone," and when the class quietened down she continued. "Well done, I've seen lots of good ideas, so we'll work on the headlines and putting it all together after lunch. Then I will choose the best reports for the display. Now, save what you have done so far, and pack your things away quietly and wait until I dismiss you."

As the class busied themselves clearing away, Mrs Jackson came over to William's table. "You three seemed to be getting on famously; have you had a good morning Parveen?"

Parveen turned to Mrs Jackson, "Yes, thank you, Mrs Jackson."

Mrs Jackson smiled. "That's good, and I hope William and Jason have looked after you and helped you to understand the story."

Parveen nodded, "Oh yes thank you, they've both been really helpful and friendly."

Chapter 18

Tommy's Revenge

Lunchtime at School, Thursday November 2nd

'Drrrriiiing, drrrriiiing', the bell sounded, and the class stopped talking and sat up straight, hoping to be dismissed first. Mrs Jackson turned to William's table and said, "Well done table five, you can go first. Katie, can you take Parveen into lunch with you please?" William pushed his chair back and held the door open for Jason's wheelchair. Then just as he turned, he saw Tommy Smithers pointing his finger at him again.

Once in the dining hall, William chose lasagne with salad and a tumbler of water for his lunch and went to find a seat. Miss Frederick met up with Jason and they went off to find a space at another table.

Once again, William was left on his own. He looked around and saw Parveen talking with Katie and her friends. They all seemed to want to talk to Parveen. At least she didn't look upset any more. William wasn't surprised; after all, she was the new girl, and the only Indian pupil in the school.

As he was sipping his water, William could see Tommy Smithers sitting at the next table. He was eating a burger, taking huge bites and talking with his mouth full. William knew that his stepdad would certainly have told him off for that. As William was watching, Tommy looked his way and then leant forward to whisper something to Johnno and Col'. They looked across at William and then burst out laughing. William suddenly felt that sick feeling starting again in his stomach.

He got up and quickly cleaned his tray before leaving the dining hall. He was so afraid that he ran down the corridor to get his coat. It was not on the hook, it was lying on the floor. It was covered in muddy footprints! His mum had only just washed it. He knew he had hung it up properly, and then he remembered Tommy's threat. This was his revenge. He must have done it when he went to the toilet. William picked it up and went outside into the playground. He could see Mrs Hudson, the playground supervisor. She always wore a shiny purple tabard with the school name on it, and today she was wearing warm-looking boots, a fur-trimmed hat and gloves. William liked Mrs Hudson; she was always smiling and seemed to be friendly.

"Hello William," she said with a cheerful smile, "I should put that coat on if I were you, it's cold out here."

William didn't answer but unfolded the coat, showing her the footprints all over it. She said, "Oh my, what a mess. Don't worry, if you go to the front office and ask Mrs Cole, I'm sure she will have a brush. You should be able to get most of it off, keep it dry now. It'll need washing tonight though."

William thanked her and returned to the main building. As he walked down the corridor, Tommy Smithers emerged from the dining hall, and he saw William carrying his coat over his arm.

"Look here Col', if it isn't Billy Boffin, Mrs Jackson's pet poodle," and the other boys sniggered. Tommy then put on a high-pitched voice like a posh lady and continued, "Oh William, what's the matter, has your coat got dirty? Oh dear, don't cry."

The other boys were now laughing and giving each other high fives. William could feel his temper building up again as he fought back the tears. He really wanted to knock that stupid grin off Tommy's face. His mum and David had warned him about losing his temper, and advised him to just walk away whenever he felt angry.

"You should try counting up to ten," his mum had said. "That will give you time to calm down." So instead of punching Tommy he went to the boys' toilets and began counting. He daren't let those boys see how upset he was.

After a little while, he rubbed his eyes and then

checked in the mirror to see if he looked as if he'd been crying. After he was satisfied that he looked okay, he made his way to the front office and tapped on the glass window. Mrs Cole wiped her hands on a napkin, and smoothed down her skirt as she got up from her desk.

William could see she'd been eating her sandwiches. William thought she always looked very nice and her hair always looked as if she'd just been to the hairdressers. As she opened the hatch, William noticed her nails were painted dark red.

She smiled and said, "Hello William, what brings you here, you look a bit upset?"

William showed her his coat, but he didn't mention Tommy Smithers. He had already been on the receiving end from Tommy. 'Grassing' on him now would only make things worse. He explained that Mrs Hudson had suggested that she might be able to help.

"Oh well, I think I can, now let me see, just wait a moment, we keep all sorts of things in that cupboard over there, just in case."

With that she went to a cupboard on the far side of the office and rummaged through a box.

William heard her exclaim, "Ah ha, there it is," returning triumphantly holding a clothes brush. "Here you are," she said, passing the brush to William, "you'd better do it outside because of the dust. When you've finished, just pop it back here." After he'd finished brushing his coat it did look a little cleaner, so he returned the brush to Mrs Cole and thanked her.

Chapter 19

More Trouble

Lunchtime, Thursday November 2nd

William zipped up his coat and went back into the playground. He scanned the pupils skipping, playing chase, climbing on the frame or playing football. He could see Parveen was chatting with a group of girls including Katie.

Tommy Smithers was standing a little way off with his gang of friends, and they were staring at Parveen. He turned and said something and the boys burst out laughing. William sensed that he'd said something rude about Parveen. That was his style. William walked slowly towards the group of girls that included Parveen and heard Tommy say in a loud voice, "Parveen, do you eat curry?" He paused before adding, "My dad says that curry looks like cow poo!"

Some children sniggered, a few gasped in shock. Parveen's face screwed up as if in pain. Almost immediately, like a pack of hunting dogs, Tommy's friends began chanting, "You eat cow poo, you eat cow…"

Parveen lunged forward grabbing for Tommy's hair. Shocked by the suddenness of her attack Tommy staggered backwards. He grappled with her and eventually broke free of her grip. Before they could continue, William charged into him, grabbing him around the waist. Tommy didn't see William coming and together they crashed to the ground. Then they began rolling around, each trying to hold the other down. Tommy wrestled his arm free and swung a hard punch which caught William on the left cheek just below his eye. It hurt a lot, but William continued to hold on tight. The children began crowding around and some had begun chanting,

"Fight… fight… fight…"

"Stop that right now! That's enough!" shouted Mrs Hudson, blowing her whistle as she came hurrying across the yard to break it up.

"Right you two, come here; the rest of you can move away, thank you."

The pupils moved a few paces back, waiting excitedly to see what would happen next.

Mrs Hudson was certainly not smiling now and she spoke in a very stern voice, "Right then boys, what on earth do you think you were doing? We can't have pupils fighting. Are either of you hurt?"

"No Miss," both boys said quickly, looking down at their feet. Neither of them was going to admit that they were wounded in any way.

William spoke up, "I'm sorry Mrs Hudson, Tommy was saying some horrid things about Parveen."

"I did not, you can ask anyone," denied Tommy angrily, "he just attacked me."

"That's enough. You can both tell Mrs Hargreaves all about it."

Mrs Hudson then spotted the mark on William's cheek. "You'd both better come with me so that we can get that looked at."

As Mrs Hudson moved off, walking in between the two boys, there was a group of pupils standing a little way off. Tommy glanced across and gave them a sly wink.

"You battered him, Tommy," called out one of the boys, hiding amongst the crowd of onlookers.

"That's enough of that," said Mrs Hudson sharply, grateful that Mr Hunt was ringing the bell to signal that lunch was over.

"Right you two. Let's go and get a 'cool pack' for that cheek William, and then we shall see what Mrs Hargreaves has to say about this."

Later, when the two boys stepped into the head teacher's office, the atmosphere was distinctly frosty. Mrs Hargreaves stood up from behind her desk and walked over to where the boys were standing with their heads bowed. William was holding a blue gel pouch against his swollen cheek. She removed her spectacles, letting them hang from a silver chain. She paused and gave a deep sigh.

"Well William, what have you got to say?"

William felt his cheeks go red as he recounted what Tommy had said. He explained why he'd felt that he should try and stop Parveen getting hurt when she lunged for Tommy. "Go on," said Mrs Hargreaves quietly.

"Well I admit, I did attack him, he was being so cruel to Parveen."

"So William, is there anything else you would like to say before I ask Tommy for his side of the story?"

William glanced across at Tommy; he thought about mentioning the footprints on his coat but decided against it. Instead, he just shrugged his shoulders and replied, "No Miss, that's the truth, I promise."

The head teacher looked at Tommy and nodded her head and so he began.

"Well," he said, "I was in the playground with Col' and Johnno and we decided to join the group talking to the new girl. I asked her if she ate curry and then William attacked me. You can ask anyone, they'll tell you."

"Why did Parveen get so upset? Are you *sure* that was what you said?" Mrs Hargreaves asked, her voice suggesting she doubted him.

"Yes Mrs Hargreaves, I didn't mean to upset her. I'm sorry if I did. I know I shouldn't have hit William, but he started it, he attacked me first. He's admitted it."

"Right," said Mrs Hargreaves, looking at Tommy, "I will need to speak to some of the pupils who witnessed everything. So who do you think I should speak to? Name someone who saw the whole thing."

"Well, Colin and Johnno were closest, they would have seen everything," responded Tommy.

Then Mrs Hargreaves looked at William. He knew that the boys would lie and cover up for Tommy. He wasn't even sure about Katie. She hardly spoke to him and once even she had called him 'Lippy', even though she knew he didn't like it.

"I think you should speak to Katie and Parveen, they were standing together and heard what he said and know what started it."

"Right, I'll speak to them later and then I'll decide what's to be done. I'm really annoyed with you both, do you understand?" She was glaring down on them both. William looked down at his scuffed shoes.

She continued, "We do not accept fighting in this school and you will be punished, you can be sure of that. Now, whilst I sort out what happened, I need to keep you separated, so William, you will go to Mr Hunt's class whilst Tommy, you will go to Mrs Anderson. When I've spoken with the other children, I will come and collect you."

As the three of them walked down the corridor towards Mrs Jackson's classroom, Mrs Hargreaves added, "I will be contacting your parents before home time, to let them know what you've been up to, do you understand?"

"Yes Mrs Hargreaves," both boys replied solemnly…

William couldn't concentrate on his work whilst he was sitting in Mr Hunt's class. His cheek was hurting and he was worried about what was going to happen. He knew David would be furious with him as soon as he found out that he'd been fighting again. He thought his mum would be very upset because he had let her down.

A few minutes before home time, Mrs Hargreaves knocked on the classroom door and entered.

"Thank you Mr Hunt, I'll take William off your hands now," she said. "Come on young man."

As William gathered up his books he felt his heart thumping in his chest. Tommy was already waiting outside her office when they arrived. Mrs Hargreaves opened the door and stood in front of the two crestfallen young boys.

"Right, I've spoken to the witnesses you suggested and now have the full picture of what happened. I'm glad I talked to Parveen first William, she spoke up for you. I now understand why you were so angry with Tommy, but you cannot go starting fights. Violence is not the right way to solve a problem, you must learn to tell someone else who will be able to sort it out."

"Yes Mrs Hargreaves, I'm sorry, it won't happen again."

"How's your cheek, you've got quite a swelling coming?" William reached up and touched his cheek gently and winced at the pain.

"It's fine," he replied, not wanting to admit how much it hurt in front of Tommy.

Then she turned to Tommy. "Tommy, what you said was cruel and spiteful, it was not funny! I believe you wanted to show off to your friends and make them laugh. You didn't care how much you upset Parveen." She paused momentarily before continuing, "I've decided that you will both be grounded at break and lunchtime tomorrow. Tommy, you will apologise to Parveen, and I have spoken to your mother so she knows all about it and she is furious with you. As for you William, I've tried to speak to your parents but their phones seem to be turned to voicemail so I've had to leave messages. I've written a letter explaining what has happened. It will be in your register before home time, now you two shake hands and give me your promises that there will be no more fighting."

William and Tommy reluctantly shook hands and returned to their class. Jason and Parveen welcomed William back with a smile as he sat down at their table. Parveen looked concerned as she mouthed, "Are you all right William?" When William nodded, she smiled again and added, "Thanks for standing up for me."

Mrs Hargreaves asked Parveen to join her in the corridor and then stood by as Tommy mumbled his apology to Parveen. "Good, now let that be the end of the matter," she said.

Jason and Parveen were keen to show William the newspaper report on Guy Fawkes that they had finished off together.

"That looks great," said William, truly impressed. Mrs Jackson joined them and quietly told William that she would speak to him at the end of school. Some of the class were staring at him. Katie Waterstone smiled at him before looking away. Tommy, Colin and Johnno ignored him.

The bell went, chairs scraped and doors opened to the sounds of children in the corridor collecting their bags, coats and lunchboxes. Mrs Jackson came over to William as he remained at the table. She wasn't smiling, but she didn't look too cross either as she gave him the envelope and said, "Make sure your parents get to see this. We know they are both at work and we have left messages on their phones. Tell them to call us tomorrow if they wish to talk to us about what happened."

"Yes, Mrs Jackson, I am sorry about fighting Tommy."

"Mrs Hargreaves has told me all about it and Parveen told me that no one else stood up for her, so what you did was very brave William. Only, you mustn't fight, you should have come and told Mrs Hudson or one of the teachers straight away, like you did this morning, do you understand?"

"Yes Mrs Jackson," William nodded.

"Good, now if you are sure you are fit enough to make your way home, I'll see you in the morning. You'll probably have a nice black eye by then, unless you're very lucky! Good night and remember no more fighting."

Chapter 20

The Letter

Later that afternoon, Thursday November 2nd

William got home and left the letter from school on the table before going upstairs to get changed. He looked in the mirror and was shocked by what he saw. His cheek was already badly swollen and the first signs of a dark, purple bruise were developing around his eye. He sighed as he booted up his computer. *At least I can win at 'Lego Batman'*, he thought, *Tommy Smithers can be the Joker and I'll batter him.* Within minutes he heard the outside door open and his mum entering the kitchen. She called upstairs, "William, are you up there?"

"Yes Mum, I'm on my computer, I'll be down in a while, okay?" he replied, not wanting to be with her when she opened the letter.

"Fine, I'll call you when I've made a hot chocolate. Oh, who's this letter from?"

"It's from school Mum, it's for you, didn't you get their message?" William called down.

"What message? I think you'd better come down straight away and tell me all about it. I'll put the kettle on and put this shopping away."

William had been dreading this. He wasn't really sure how his mum would react. Would she be really cross with him for fighting, or disappointed in him for getting involved, and not counting to ten? Would she be on his side when David got home? After all, William was pretty certain how he would react.

Reluctantly he logged off from his computer and then slowly made his way downstairs. His mum was busy putting things in the fridge with her back to him.

She turned around and exclaimed, "Good grief son! Who did that to you?" She rushed around the table. "Here, let me have a proper look."

"Don't get upset, Mum, I'm fine," said William, pulling away as she peered at his swollen cheek.

"We need to get some ice on that straight away to stop that swelling coming up and then you can tell me what on earth has been going on."

William told his mum the whole story as she held the kitchen towel with ice cubes wrapped in it against his cheek. He admitted to her that he had attacked Tommy first. She asked him what Mrs Hargreaves had done about Tommy. She even asked if the new girl was hurt. When he had finished telling the story and answering her questions she picked up the phone in the hall and then checked her mobile phone. Sure enough, there were a number of messages waiting for her from Mrs Hargreaves. She pressed the play button and listened as Mrs Hargreaves briefly explained what had taken place. When the message ended she read the letter.

It explained that William and Tommy had both been grounded for fighting. Mrs Hargreaves had added her concern that this was not the first time that William had been involved in 'fisticuffs'. Finally she suggested that she or David would be welcome to contact the school if they felt it necessary…

Chapter 21

My 'Big Sleep' Is Disturbed

Later that afternoon, Thursday November 2nd

Meanwhile, over in the field behind the orchard, I awoke with a start. I stirred from a deep, deep sleep, stretching out my legs and yawning. Then I listened carefully as I slowly opened my eyes. I could hear a machine in the distance which was getting louder and louder as it got nearer. It was making a terrifying noise. I was afraid that it was coming to destroy my new den. Suddenly, the machine made a loud rattling sound and then the noise stopped, and I could hear voices. Did they know I was here? Were they looking for me? Then my den started shaking, the piles of sticks and wood started swaying and creaking. Were they coming to get me? Was it those boys again? I curled up into a tight ball fearing for my life.

"Johnno, can you stick those pallets around the

bottom please, they're just the job," a man's voice said.

"Okay," replied a younger voice, "I cannot wait till Sunday, it's going to be brilliant. Can I ask some of my friends to come over?"

"You'll have to ask your mum about that, but I don't see why not…"

The chinks of light were soon blocked out by the extra wood that was added and my den now became totally dark.

The man spoke again, "It's done us a good turn, being bonfire night. I've tidied up the barn and got rid of all that old wood. Now come on, it's getting cold and it'll be dark in an hour and the cows won't milk themselves."

The machine roared into life, clanking and knocking loudly, and then began to move away. I started to calm down as the danger seemed to have passed and before long I relaxed back into my deep sleep……

Chapter 22
More Explaining To Do

Early evening, Thursday November 2nd

David came home much later, by which time William was back in his room on his computer. He'd left the door open so that he could hear what his mum and stepdad were saying in the kitchen below.

He overheard David say in an angry voice, "No lad of ours is going to get a reputation for being a troublemaker. I'm going to have a word with him."

His mum replied calmly, "Yes David, I understand, but if what he said is true, he stood up for that poor girl against that horrible boy; I think he did the right thing!"

"We can't allow him to take the law into his own hands, so we need to nip this in the bud before he gets older, bigger and stronger, and that is when people really do get hurt. Trust me! I've seen it in my school, when a couple of year elevens 'kick off'." He paused for a moment before adding, "And the girls can be just as bad."

"David, have a word with him, if you must, but remember, he did what he thought was right," said his mum.

"Fine," replied David brusquely, "Margaret, leave this to me."

Moments later there was a sharp knock on William's bedroom door and David walked straight in. "Young man, your mum's been telling me about your fight today." He bent forward to get a closer look at the swelling by William's eye. "Judging by your face, it looks like it was quite a scrap."

"Not really. I just got mad when I heard Tommy Smithers say those disgusting things about the new girl, Parveen, and her family."

"I understand that William, but fighting doesn't make things right. You should have reported it to one of the teachers, or the playground supervisor. Let them deal with it."

"I did David, honest, I did, at break time," implored William, and he went on to tell him about Tommy's threats and his coat.

"Okay William, I believe you, but you must promise me you won't get into a fight again, and that you'll go and tell someone and let them sort it out."

"I'll promise, David, but if somebody was being cruel to mum or me what would you do?"

David hesitated for a moment before replying, "Fair point son, just make sure you control your temper and don't be the one to start it, do you understand the difference?" William nodded before David continued, "Right, I want you to write a letter to Mrs Hargreaves telling her that you promise not to start any more fights in the future. You can take it to school in the morning. I'll give her a ring in the morning just to make sure the matter is closed."

"Yes David. I am sorry about fighting and thank you for believing me and not shouting at me."

"Okay, let's leave it there, something smells really good, which must mean tea is ready. Let's go before we both get into your mum's bad books…"

Chapter 23

A Big Surprise

After tea, Thursday November 2nd

Back in his bedroom, William was trying to write the letter to Mrs Hargreaves.

"Not on your computer," David had insisted, "as it will look like your Mum or I have done it." William had started it several times, but each time he either made a mistake or it looked really untidy. His handwriting looked so spidery that David would probably make him do it again anyway. He was feeling really fed up when there was a knock on his bedroom door and his mum entered.

"I've come to see how you're getting on. I thought you might want a hot chocolate for some inspiration," she said, her voice teasing him gently as she noticed several balls of writing paper screwed up by the bin.

"It's too hard, Mum, I just don't know what to say," William said in frustration.

"I can't promise it won't happen again. If I see someone upsetting or hurting someone else, it makes me really mad. I can't help it. I am sorry Mum, but I know how I feel when they call me Lippy and Billy Boffin, I try to ignore it and count to ten like you said, but it still hurts inside."

His mum turned him towards her and hugged him tightly. "It's okay to feel hurt and angry son, but just promise me, you will tell the teachers."

"That will just make things worse. The kids will just call me 'grasser' and gang up on me."

"No son, please listen to me; how could it make it any worse? They are already upsetting you all the time and they believe there's nothing you can do about it. That's exactly what the bullies want you to think. If you don't tell anyone, they can carry on doing it because nobody knows what is happening. It is a secret," she said.

William's mum hesitated as the telephone rang, waiting to see if David would answer it and then, after a moment, she continued. "Once you tell somebody about what is going on, they lose that power over you. They know they cannot get away with it any longer. The secret is out and they know they will be in trouble if they continue to be horrible."

"Okay Mum, we'll see if Tommy behaves himself and leaves me alone," William replied doubtfully.

William's mum hugged him again and said,

"Good, now let's get this letter drafted. What do you think you should say? Then you can write it out in your best handwriting."

William had just got started once more when David called up the stairs.

"Can you both come down here a moment please? I have something to tell you."

They looked at each other and William's mum shrugged her shoulders in puzzlement before they stood up and went downstairs and into the living room.

David was standing with his back to the fireplace, warming himself. William's mum sat on the settee and patted the cushion beside her, encouraging William to join her.

"Right, now you're sitting comfortably, I'll begin," David said, smiling at his own joke. "That was Mr Bedi, Parveen's father, on the phone. Parveen has just told him what happened at school today. He is very grateful to you William for being so kind to her and so very brave, standing up to those boys. He also told me how proud we should be to have a son who would do such a thing, particularly standing up for a stranger. He insisted that we all go to their house on Sunday night for dinner. He says his wife is an excellent cook."

"What did you say?" asked William's mum. "It's bonfire night on Sunday and I thought we'd watch the Taylors' fireworks, from our bedroom window. If the bonfire is anything to go by it should be quite a show. I've even bought a few fireworks for you to let off in the orchard."

"Well, we can do that on another night. Mr Bedi, was insistent, and it would have seemed rude to refuse. He said they would expect us to arrive about seven o'clock."

"That's really kind of them, where do they live? I've never been to an Indian family's house before. It will be really interesting; do we need to take anything? I hope the food is not too spicy though," William's mum babbled on excitedly.

"Slow down, Margaret, slow down. It is their way of saying thank you to William. He hoped he hadn't got into too much trouble. I told him that the school had dealt with it fairly so the matter was closed. Now we've sorted that out, how is that letter coming along son?" asked David with a serious look on his face.

"Getting there, I'm just going to put some food out for Lucky before I finish it off," replied William, getting up from the sofa.

"Oh William, before you do that," said David with a beaming smile on his face, "Mr Bedi was absolutely right; you are a special young man and your mum and I are both very proud of you."

William felt his cheeks blush with embarrassment. "Thanks," he mumbled, before adding awkwardly, "Dad."

Chapter 24

I Begin My 'Big Sleep'

Late that night, Thursday November 2nd

Meanwhile, in my new nest in the meadow beyond the orchard, I was busy rearranging the pile of leaves to build up my bed, tugging them into just the right place. It was amongst a huge pile of wooden boards, tree branches and cardboard boxes. After my lucky escape last time I made sure that there were no foxes or other monsters already hiding in there. It seemed to be absolutely perfect for my big sleep. The night air felt cold. The icy wind had woken me up, as it howled and whistled between the pieces of wood. The branches creaked and groaned above me. I snuggled down, curling up tightly into a ball. In my mind I could picture William, and I imagined him holding me gently in those thick gloves. I felt sad at the thought that I would never see him again. He had behaved just like our mum, one minute looking after me, the next gone for ever. As I remembered his last words to me, "Be lucky", my eyelids were feeling really heavy and I must have drifted into a deep, deep sleep…

Chapter 25

A Good Day

All day at school, Friday November 3rd

William swallowed his final mouthful of 'Wheatie Crisps' and gulped down his orange juice.

"Have you put everything ready for school? Don't forget the letter for Mrs Hargreaves. You put it on the mantelpiece," his mum reminded him.

"Okay Mum, I won't,"

"Come on William, grab your coat, you don't want to be late, especially today," called his mum.

At school, for once, William had a good day. He handed the letter to Mrs Hargreaves and, after she'd read it, she thanked him and told him that the matter was now closed as far as she was concerned.

After taking the register, Mrs Jackson informed

the class that there was going to be a special assembly. She then dismissed the class one table at a time to go to the main hall.

As the children entered and settled down in neat rows, Mrs Hargreaves was standing on the stage at the front with her arms folded. The assembly began as usual with a prayer and the children sang a song with Mr Hunt playing the piano. Then the children sat down again and Mrs Hargreaves began.

"Now boys and girls, as it is Guy Fawkes Night this weekend, we've got a special visitor with us this morning. I expect many of you will be going to a fireworks party either at home or at friend's so I've invited a leading firefighter, Graham Stark, to give us some advice to make sure that we have a nice time and we all stay safe. Please welcome him with a nice round of applause to make him feel welcome."

As the applause died down the firefighter made his way to the stage carrying two metal buckets. One was filled with some clean water and the other was filled with some sand.

"Good morning children. How many of you will be going to a fireworks party over the next few days?" he asked. Most of the children raised their hands.

"Now how many of you will be holding one of these?" he asked, holding up some sparklers. Again many hands shot up into the air.

"Who thinks these fireworks are really just for young children, after all they seem pretty harmless?" Once again, many hands were raised. "Well let's see shall we?" He began scanning the pupils' faces as they looked at him with eager anticipation before turning to Johnno and asking, "Young man, what's your name?"

"Johnno."

"Johnno, how would you like to join me up here and give me a hand please?" Johnno stood up immediately with a beaming smile and quickly joined the firefighter on the stage. Then the firefighter saw Parveen and invited her to join them on stage.

"Right, to make sure you're safe, first of all you must have a pair of these," he said, passing a pair of gloves to Johnno and Parveen who quickly popped them on. Next, he took two thick plastic tubes out of his pocket and asked the pair of them to try and snap them in half. The excited pupils in the audience leaned forward to watch and were surprised when Johnno said, "It's too strong, I can't do it."

"Well thank you both for trying. Now children, I want you to imagine that these tubes are your fingers and let's see what happens."

Turning to Parveen he said, "Ladies first," as he gave her a sparkler to hold in her gloved hand and then passed one to Johnno. "Now boys and girls, these sparklers are special indoor ones, but even these can give you a serious burn if you are not very careful." He whispered something to Johnno and Parveen and demonstrated exactly how they should stand with the sparkler held at arm's length. Taking out a cigarette lighter he lit Parveen's sparkler and within seconds it was hissing and spitting bright sparks as she waved it about in small circles sending sparks shooting outwards.

After a little while the sparks spluttered and stopped and Graham invited Parveen to hold her sparkler against the plastic tube. It quickly melted through the tubing, slicing through it easily. There was a gasp from the pupils as they saw just how hot the remaining metal rod had become.

"Now, imagine that was the skin melting off your hand or a finger. You'd be off to the hospital and scarred for life." He paused momentarily as many of the children went 'urghh' in horror at the thought.

"Parveen, could you place that sparkler into that bucket of water please." As the sparkler was plunged into the water it hissed and steam formed a smoky cloud.

"Now children, can you see how hot that still is?"

"Now Johnno, it's your turn."

Once again the sparkler sliced through the tube.

"So children, that shows you what happens to your skin if you get burned and why I'm here today, to warn you all, PLEASE, NEVER, EVER MESS ABOUT WITH FIRE OR FIREWORKS!" he said in a strong, clear voice.

Mrs Hargreaves stepped forward and reminded the children about the key points and thanked Johnno and Parveen for being such good demonstrators.

The head teacher then told the pupils that they should look out for one another and not say nasty or spiteful things about each other. She explained that if anyone was being nasty and saying cruel things, she expected them to let a teacher know straight away. She warned that such behaviour would not be

109

tolerated and that the pupils involved would be in serious trouble.

Back in her classroom, Mrs Jackson announced that the story William, Jason and Parveen had produced, was going to be one of the centrepieces of the Guy Fawkes display in the main corridor. As William and Tommy were both grounded in separate classrooms during break and lunchtime, it meant that William had no more trouble from him. A few of the pupils asked him about his black eye, but only out of concern. Not one person teased him or called him Lippy or Billy Boffin. A couple of girls even said how brave he was for standing up to Tommy Smithers, which made him feel much better. He felt his face was going red with embarrassment.

Parveen didn't mention anything about him going to her house until the end of school. However, when she had finished buttoning her blue padded coat she smiled at him and said casually, "See you on Sunday."

William felt very embarrassed so he simply mumbled, "Yes, great, see you then."

Chapter 26
Getting Ready For His Big Day

Tea-time at home, Friday November 3rd

"Right then son, are your clothes all ready for tomorrow morning? Do I need to wash or iron anything?" asked his mum.

"No thanks Mum, they're fine," he replied.

"You'll need a pullover and your coat too. You could wear that one as it's getting much colder. Now, are your wellies clean? You don't want to turn up in dirty wellies."

David added, "Don't forget, I said I'll drop you off at the surgery in the morning just before ten, on my way to school. I'd like to have a word with Mr Wilson anyway. Then I'll pop into school to support the boys. It's the semi-final of the East District Under-15s Cup."

"Thanks David, I'm feeling a bit tired now so I'll just put some food out for Lucky, in case she's hungry, and then go up to my room and read awhile."

"Good night son, and don't forget to apologise to Mr Wilson for giving him such a fright," his mum said.

William went into the kitchen, took down a new tin of the chicken-flavoured cat food. He opened it and forked some into the same bowl he'd used the night before, carefully placing it on the pathway under the garage door light.

Chapter 27

William's Lucky Break

Breakfast time, Saturday November 4th

The next morning, as William munched his way through his 'Wheatie Crisps,' cereal, his mum said, "I've put you some sandwiches, an apple, that new chocolate bar you like and a bottle of orange juice for your lunch, so that should keep you going."

"That sounds great, thanks Mum,"

"Hey come on, the roads are slippery today," David said impatiently as he glanced at his watch. "It will take us longer to get there."

"Now, here's your coat and scarf, be good and have a good time," his mum said, before turning to David. "What time do you think you'll be back?"

"I don't know, I'll speak to Mr Wilson and call you."

With that he gave William's mum another one of those little kisses on the cheek. "See you later love, bye…"

Throughout the journey William sat quietly, looking out at the hedgerows and fields coated in a silvery frost. He was thinking about Lucky and wondering where she might be. Was she safe? Was she getting enough to eat? The surface of the road sparkled in the crisp, morning air. The fields appeared to be steaming in the pale sunlight and there was a layer of ground mist covering them.

Suddenly, his thoughts were interrupted as David spoke. "I think the match at school may have to be called off with all this frost, and so I'll drop you off and get on my way to school. Some of the lads may need lifts or parents contacting."

William realised he didn't need to reply; he had been worrying about what Mr Wilson was going to say about nearly running him over on Wednesday night.

Moments later, the car turned into the small car park in front of the vets' surgery. There were a few cars lined up, including the large red car that William now knew belonged to Mr Wilson. The surgery was in a big old house on the edge of Croxton. David pushed open the door labelled 'Waiting Room'.

A woman wearing a green tunic was wiping down the reception desk and there was a really strong smell of fresh disinfectant. William remembered her from when he'd visited for one of Lucky's check-ups.

"Oh hello, can I help you?" she asked.

David replied, "Oh, yes please, this is William; Mr Wilson has kindly offered him the chance to help with the animals. Is he available?"

The lady smiled. "Oh hello again William, I remember you, you rescued that poor hedgehog. Goodness me you look like you've been in the wars with that eye. Is it very painful?" she asked.

William smiled, "No it's not too bad today, thank you."

"My name's Helen, but you probably guessed that as it says so on my badge."

She then looked at David. "I'm sorry, Mr Wilson left early in the jeep. He's been called out to a mare that is having difficulty foaling. Don't worry though, we are expecting William. Mr Wilson left me clear instructions about what he would like him to do. I am to give him a tour around and then he's going to work with Mrs Wilson in the Rescue Centre today."

William couldn't believe his luck! With Mr Wilson out and David in a hurry to get to school, it meant that they weren't going to talk about the incident in the road on Wednesday night. Phew, how lucky was that?

"Oh, right," said David. "That's okay; William's got his lunch with him. What time should I collect him this afternoon?"

"Oh, anytime around three. There's no surgery tonight, so once the morning surgery is finished we just make sure that any animals to be collected have gone home and their cages have been cleaned and disinfected."

"That'll be fine, thank you." David then turned to

William. "Now be good and mind your manners. See you later then, bye," and with that he left.

"Right then, William, You come with me and I'll get you fitted out with one of our green sweatshirts. We don't want that lovely pullover getting dirty do we?"

William waited as Helen unlocked a cupboard and removed a brand new green sweatshirt. She held it up against him and said, "There you are, put that on; it's a bit big but it should do the job."

"Wow, thank you, it's lovely," said William as Helen tugged at the sleeves and straightened it until she was satisfied with the fit. He followed her through to the back of the centre. She showed him the room where Mr Wilson examined the animals, and next to it was the surgery where he carried out the operations. Just along the corridor was the recovery room. It was here that he'd first seen Lucky after the operation on her jaw. William could still remember everything about that day and being there made him wonder what Lucky was doing at this very moment.

Next, Helen introduced him to Sue, Mr Wilson's assistant. "Sue, William's here to give Mrs Wilson a hand at the Rescue Centre."

Sue glanced up from the form she was filling in and smiled. "Oh hello William, it's nice to see you again. How's Lucky doing, have you seen her since her release?"

"No I haven't, but she's eating the food I put out for her at night, so she must still be around."

"That's good," Sue said. "I'm sorry to be rude

but I must get on, as I need to have everything ready for when Mr Wilson gets back."

"Come on then William, let's allow Sue to get on with her work," Helen said, leading William past a room filled with small animal cages next to a storeroom. Finally they came to the back door which William discovered led outside to the Animal Rescue Centre.

They went outside and down a short path before opening a farm gate into the paddock. Mrs Wilson was putting some hay into a feed rack for the horses. She was wearing jeans and a thick blue fleece with the Rescue Centre logo on the front. William watched as the pair of hungry horses trotted over to feed and immediately began pulling at the hay. Mrs Wilson patted them both on the neck and said a few words to them both before turning away and striding across the muddy paddock to where William and Helen were waiting.

She greeted William with a friendly smile. "Hello, you must be William. My name's Carol, and Peter's told me a lot about you; you're here to give me a hand this morning I believe?"

"Yes," answered William politely, "I want to learn how to look after sick animals when I'm older. I would like to become a vet like Mr Wilson one day."

"Well then, you've come to the right place to learn. What I think we should do is let you meet the animals first. I'll tell you a bit about them and then you can give me a hand cleaning them out, feeding them and making sure that they are okay."

William quickly decided that he liked helping Mrs Wilson. She had a smiley face and her eyes twinkled when she spoke to him. She looked a bit younger than his mum and slimmer. He noticed she was wearing red lipstick, but his mum only put that on when she was going to work or they were going out. The time passed by very quickly as she told him about all the animals. First were the two horses, Holly and Molly, which Mrs Wilson and her daughter Charlene rode every day.

Next were the two very old donkeys named Trixie and Jenny that used to give children rides on the sands at Weston-super-Mare. They were much too old for that now and sadly Trixie had gone blind. Trixie relied upon Jenny to help her to find her way around. Mrs Wilson told William to be careful not to startle them, but talk to them, from a little way off. She gave him a piece of carrot to feed them and then said, "Watch me first, I'll show you." She called to the donkeys, "Hello Jenny, hello Trixie, come on then, come on then." Jenny lifted her head and looked in their direction as if weighing up if it was worth the effort to walk over. After a few moments Mrs Wilson said softly, "Come on Jenny, come on Trixie, look what we've got for you."

Jenny began to plod slowly towards them. Trixie hesitated and then, as if by remote control, she turned and began plodding alongside her faithful friend. Mrs Wilson held out the carrot and Jenny snuffled her hand before taking it from her. Trixie had stopped and Mrs Wilson spoke again. "Here you are Trixie old girl, a nice carrot for you," and the donkey stepped forward, snuffling her hand before accepting the treat.

"You can stroke them gently but do watch their hooves. They can step on your toes if you are not careful." As William began to stroke Jenny, the donkey turned her head and her lips curled up revealing her large, brown, stained teeth. Startled, William jumped back out of the way.

"It's okay, William," Mrs Wilson said with a chuckle, "the old girl was checking to see if you had another carrot in your pocket. They can give you a painful nip if you are not careful. It is always safer to put their treats on the floor. It saves you from getting bitten because to a donkey, a carrot and a finger look the same."

Mrs Wilson offered another carrot to Trixie, wafting it by her nose before placing it on the floor for her to pick up. After stroking the pair for a couple of minutes they moved on.

William counted twelve brown chickens pecking around by the hay racks and 'gossiping' to each other. At least that's what Mrs Wilson said they were doing as the birds made their, 'chuck... chuck... chuck' clucking sounds. William thought they looked really funny as their heads bobbed forwards jerkily as they walked. They picked their feet up very slowly and then placed them down carefully as if their feet were really sore. Their eyes were never still as they sought out any tiny seeds of grain on the floor and then jabbed down quickly with their beaks. Meanwhile, across the paddock, William could see some white geese. They were all waddling in the same direction, sticking close together in a group.

"Safety in numbers," Mrs Wilson explained to him. "Now let's go inside and see who is in there."

As they walked towards the Rescue Centre, William realised it was housed in the old stable block. William was surprised how old and rickety it looked. The roof was covered by tin sheets, some of which were rusty, and the white paint on the brick walls was peeling and flaking off. The weathered doors were split into two sections to allow the top half to be opened whilst not letting the occupants out. Mrs Wilson unbolted one of the doors and stepped inside. William was immediately struck by the smell. Not disinfectant this time, but the sweet grass smell of the hay bales stacked in the corner. Bedding straw was stacked in the other corner. The room was split up into a series of pens made by using wooden rails with wire netting running along the bottom bars.

In the first pen a small fox was curled up in an old dog basket. "Oh wow, a fox cub, that's awesome," exclaimed William. "I've never seen a fox cub before. I didn't expect to see one this close up. Why does it look so sad?" he asked.

Mrs Wilson explained that they suspected that this cub's mother had been run over on the bypass.

"It is very unusual to see such a small fox cub at this time of the year. I suspect his mum died a few days ago and this little fellow wasn't able to feed himself."

Mrs Wilson told him that a farmer's wife had

found the cub yesterday, asleep in their barn. "He looked as if he was close to starving to death. She'd given him some warm milk but she couldn't keep him because they had two farm dogs and she daren't tell her husband about it as he certainly wouldn't want a fox around the farm!" She added that they hadn't given it a name yet and William made her laugh when he said that they should call the fox 'Reedy' after one of the boys in his class who also had very orangey brown hair.

There were five dogs of various ages and breeds, and six cats plus two litters of tiny kittens who mewed as they tumbled over each other playfully. Mrs Wilson explained to William that all the animals had been brought to the Rescue Centre to be looked after because they'd been badly treated, become ill, or perhaps their owners just couldn't cope with them anymore. She added that it was her job to try and find them good homes where they could have a better life and where they would be loved and properly cared for. When they had finished putting the new bedding into the kittens' pen, Mrs Wilson exclaimed, "Goodness William, look at the time. We'll stop now; we need to wash our hands thoroughly with the disinfectant soap, then you can have your sandwiches, Helen told me you'd brought some."

William had been so busy and having such a great time he hadn't had time to feel hungry. "Wow, that's gone quickly, time doesn't go that fast at school," he said.

"You can eat your lunch with Sue. I want to have

a chat with Peter and then we'll finish off. It should only take us half an hour or so. Helen told me that your dad's coming at around three and we will easily be done by then."

William did not feel like explaining to Mrs Wilson that David was not his real dad, so he went to find Sue.

Chapter 28

William Gets A Warning

Lunchtime, Saturday November 4th

Sue was still doing paperwork and didn't seem to want to talk, so William sat quietly eating his sandwiches. His mum had put a little note in with them saying that she hoped he was having a nice time. His mum always stood up for him whenever David was annoyed with him and she would always try to make him feel better if he was upset. As he sat quietly, he decided to give his mum an extra-special hug when he got home to say 'thank you'.

Just then, Mr Wilson came bustling into the room. "Well then young William, Carol tells me what a nuisance you've been this morning." William was shocked and wondered what he had done

123

wrong. Then he noticed Mr Wilson was smiling. He was teasing him. Adults do that a lot, he thought, and it certainly isn't the same as the spiteful name-calling and upsetting bullying that children do to each other.

Mr Wilson added, "I hope everyone has been looking after you."

William finished chewing a mouthful of apple before replying, "Oh yes, everyone has been really nice and it's been really interesting, thank you."

"Now I need to have a little word with you, in private; just follow me into my office." With that he turned and left the room. William trailed behind; he could guess what was coming. He was dreading the telling-off he felt sure he was about to get. Mr Wilson closed the door before sitting down at his desk.

"Now then William, what on earth were you doing in the middle of the road, I almost killed you?" he said sharply.

William decided it would be best to tell the truth and so he explained about how he had been looking for Lucky. He'd seen the dead hedgehog in the road and was checking to see if it was her.

He added, "I'm really sorry, I didn't hear you coming, it won't happen again, I promise."

"Ah, so that was it, at least now I understand," and he gave a big sigh. "I was pretty shaken up I can tell you."

"I'm really sorry," said William, "please don't tell my mum or David that I was looking for Lucky, they'll be really mad at me," he pleaded.

"Okay, we'll say no more about it. Are you putting food out for Lucky as I suggested?"

"Yes, her favourite cat food, it was all gone this morning, I'm sure she is still around."

"You can't be sure it's Lucky, William, as it could be a cat or a fox that's coming for the food." said Mr Wilson. He was quiet for a moment before he continued, "Tell you what, I'll show you how to make a hedgehog feeding station if you like."

"Wow, thanks," replied William enthusiastically.

Mr Wilson took some paper out of a drawer and selected a pencil from the holder on his desk. He drew a picture of how to place the shallow food container under a garden slab or plastic lid off a storage box supported by bricks.

"You should try putting a few mealworms out for her with a small amount of the cat food," he said. "They sell mealworms in the pet shop in the village and at the 'bargain store'. Hedgehogs love them, and so do blackbirds and robins."

"How will I know if it's Lucky that's eating them?" asked William.

"That's a really good question. Firstly, you will need to put them out after dark, when the birds have gone to sleep for the night. Then, before it gets light the next morning, you will need to check to see if anything has eaten the worms. That way, you will know that the most likely thing to have eaten the mealworms will be a hedgehog, but you will have to get up early because blackbirds wake up at dawn."

"Oh, that's such a neat idea; I'll do that tonight.

It would be wonderful to see Lucky again and know that she was doing well," said William smiling.

"William, one last thing, promise me you won't go trying to find Lucky again, as your chances of seeing her are virtually nil. Your best chance is to encourage her to come to your feeding station, but remember we want her to sleep during the winter." He glanced at his watch. "Now, I must check on the animals I operated on yesterday and I bet Carol is waiting for you, so off you go…"

For the rest of the afternoon William couldn't really concentrate, and he kept checking the time. He couldn't wait to get some mealworms from the pet shop. Then when he got home he could make a hedgehog feeding station and put the worms out for Lucky.

It wasn't long before David arrived and William dashed to get his coat from the back room. When he returned, Mr Wilson and David were talking. "He's been a real nuisance, please take him away," said Mr Wilson. William realised that he was teasing again.

David smiled and said, "Mr Wilson tells me you are a natural with the animals."

"Indeed, Mrs Wilson tells me what a big help you've been this afternoon, cleaning out the pens and putting in new bedding. Would you like to come again, next week?" Mr Wilson asked.

"Oh yes please, that would be brilliant; I can come, can't I?" said William, turning to look up at his stepdad.

"I should think so, but we'd better check with your mum first," he replied.

William gave a little jump for joy before asking, "Can we call at the pet shop please? We need to get some mealworms for Lucky; Mr Wilson said hedgehogs love them."

"Yes if you want to. Now William, have you got everything?" asked David as he reached out and shook Mr Wilson's hand.

Chapter 29

The Hedgehog Feeding Station

Late afternoon, Saturday November 4th

It only took a few minutes for David and William to arrive at the pet shop. As they entered, William recognised the now familiar smell of hay. There were several cages with rabbits, budgies, hamsters and an aquarium with tiny, brilliantly-coloured fish. There were shelves stacked with cans of dog and cat food. On the floor were dog baskets of various sizes and shapes, wire cages and mats. William ignored it all. He went straight to the section labelled 'Wild Bird Feed'. There were different kinds of bird feeders and nest boxes on display and a huge range of seeds and fat balls. He scoured the shelves and suddenly he saw what he was searching for. There, in a sealed tub, 'Dried Mealworms'. There was a picture of a blackbird and a robin on the label. "This must be it," he said, passing the tub to David.

"I'm sure your mother will love having these in the house," David joked as they went to the counter to pay. "Are you sure hedgehogs like these as they look truly disgusting?"

Before he could reply the young assistant behind the counter said, "They are gross, but at least they don't wriggle and smell like the maggots the fishermen buy!"

On the way home, David asked William if he had apologised to Mr Wilson for almost causing a terrible accident and then he asked him about his day. Although William answered politely, his mind was elsewhere; he was just thinking about setting up the feeding station for Lucky with the mealworms.

As soon as they walked into the house, his mum immediately put the kettle on to make William a hot chocolate.

"Wow, look at you in your smart sweatshirt. Now tell me all about it. Have you had a good time? Did you get to feed any animals? Were the people friendly? Did you help Mr Wilson? You must have a bath before tea after being with all those animals. I've bought some special anti-bacterial soap and shampoo."

She was speaking so quickly that David interrupted her. "Goodness Margaret, give the lad a chance."

William answered all her questions in between

sipping his chocolate. Then his mum said, "Son, we are both really proud of how you have done today." Making his mum proud made him feel good inside, almost better than the chocolate.

William couldn't wait to get to work on the feeding station, so as soon as he'd finished his drink he thanked his mum and started to go upstairs. Remembering the 'special hug' he wanted to give her for the note in his lunchbox, he turned around, stepped forward to give her a big hug and said, "Thanks for the note, Mum."

"That's lovely, son, now go and run that bath, we don't want you getting any germs off those animals," said his mum.

William ran the bath and quickly got in after leaving his clothes in a pile on the bedroom floor. After a quick soak, William 'booted up' his computer whilst he dried himself. It soon whirred into life and then he was looking at hedgehog websites. He was looking for hedgehog houses, just like Mr Wilson had described. He saw some beautiful ones, but they were really expensive, when suddenly he came across a site which showed you how to make a hedgehog house out of a plastic box.

"Wow, perfect," he muttered. "That is just what I need for Lucky."

Setting to work straight away, he pulled out a large plastic box from under his table. It was full of books, DVDs and computer games. He tipped them out onto his bed. When it was empty he turned it round in his hands, looking at it from every angle. Then he went into his mum's bedroom and carefully removed his mum's extra-large scissors out of her sewing box. He began to try to cut out a square entrance hole.

It was really difficult and he had to use both hands on the scissors to cut through the brittle plastic. Eventually, a jagged piece broke away and the entrance was made. He was disappointed that the plastic had split so badly, leaving a very ragged edge. He couldn't leave it like that, because if he did, Lucky might get injured. He wondered how he could tidy up the rough edge. He would need some tape. First he tried 'Sellotape' but it wouldn't stick properly. He needed some strong, thick tape. Then William recalled David repairing one of his bird feeders, which had been chewed by a squirrel, using some thick black tape.

"Now where would he keep that tape?" William muttered to himself. He decided that the most likely place would be in the garage.

He was just about to open the back door to go and look for it, when his mum called to him, "Oh William, you're not going out are you? Tea will be ready in five minutes."

"Won't be long Mum, I just need to get something," he replied, stepping out through the door. Once inside the garage, William realised immediately that he was faced with another problem. David had parked the car so close to the wall of shelves there was only a narrow gap on the passenger side. William squeezed himself into the tiny space, inching himself between the shelves and the side of the car. Then, leaning back against the car, he levered himself up and started to search through the racks of tools and old paint tins, white spirit, oil, car polish and de-icer cans stacked on the shelves. '*Where is it?*' he wondered. He reached out and carefully moved some of the cans aside to see if the tape was hidden behind them.

"Yes! There it is," he muttered to himself. Unfortunately it was on the top shelf behind a plastic can of oil and some old paint tins. He stretched up to try and get hold of it but his fingertips could only brush against its smooth surface…

"William, what on earth are you doing up there?" David shouted from the garage door. William jerked backwards, pulling his hand away from the tape as if he'd been stung by a wasp. His elbow knocked into a large paint tin, which in turn dislodged several others, causing them to tumble off the shelves. The plastic can of oil fell bouncing against the angle of the car door and the roof, causing the cap to fly off sending a shower of thick green oil splattering around him onto the car. William stared, horrified as he watched it oozing down the paintwork onto his jeans.

"Arrrghh, I'm sorry. I didn't mean to, I was just…… " the words gushed out of his mouth in a garbled apology.

"Oh, for goodness sake, now look what you've done!" David exclaimed. "What a flipping mess!" The oil was spreading in a slimy film down the windows onto the paintwork of his car. William was now completely stuck. He couldn't get past it without smearing it on his clothes and making it even worse.

David's face flushed bright red as he raged, "William, what is the matter with you? Why can't you leave my things alone?"

William felt the tears welling up and, although he tried not to, he began to sniffle. Just then, his mum appeared at the doorway.

"Tea's ready. Oh good grief William! What have you been up to this time?" she said, as she took in the scene.

William sniffed and wiped his nose with his arm. He was in a proper mess in more ways than one. "I'm really sorry, I just wanted to get some tape for Lucky's house," he replied.

"Just look at my car," David shouted. "That flipping hedgehog, I wish you'd never set eyes on it." His eyes were squeezed shut as if in pain, his voice was harsh and William knew he really meant it.

William's mum's hands covered her mouth in horror. "Oh David, don't say that, you know how he feels about Lucky." Then she turned to William. "Now let's get you out of there and cleaned up."

"What a mess, just look at the paintwork. It had better not be damaged my lad or you'll pay for this," David said angrily.

"Now David, that's enough; shouting will get us nowhere. Find some rags and let's get him out of there," instructed William's mum.

David strode around to the front of the car and rummaged in some drawers, returning with a handful of old cloths and towels. Then he carefully picked up the paint tins and the bottle of oil with his fingertips making sure that they didn't drip on his clothes.

It was a very tense few minutes as William tried to squeeze himself down onto the floor between the car and the shelves. David kept warning him to be careful not to scratch the paintwork. Eventually, William was free, and his mum told him to get out of his oily clothes straight away. She wrapped him in an old picnic rug before gingerly picking up his clothes, holding them well away from her own clothes.

"These are probably ruined but I'll give them a good soak. Now get yourself washed and then we can have tea. If we don't eat soon, it won't be fit to eat," she said, obviously very upset, before turning around and storming out.

William was in serious trouble.

"You're going straight to bed after tea," David said, jabbing his finger at him, "and you'll be spending tomorrow cleaning the car, do you hear me?"

Tea was eaten in silence, apart from the occasional 'please' and 'thank you' when the ketchup bottle was passed.

"Now then young man, straight to bed for you and no pocket money for a month," David said sternly.

William started to apologise again, "I'm really sor….."

"That's enough," David said, holding his hand up, "now get upstairs and if I catch you looking for that hedgehog tonight I'll take your computer off you for good and you'll never go to the Rescue Centre again, you mark my words."

"Yes David," answered William. He was feeling

absolutely wretched as he pushed his chair away from the table and went to his mum, "I'm really sorry about the trousers Mum, good night."

"Good night, son, it's done now, so let's leave it at that," she replied.

When William opened the bedroom door, the books, games and the plastic hedgehog house were still scattered on the duvet. He picked up his mother's scissors and, creeping along the landing, he returned them, exactly as he'd found them. That way she'd never know he'd used them. He was in enough trouble as it was.

Next, he quickly stuck everything back into the plastic box, before changing into his pyjamas. As he lay in bed, he went over the events of the day. What great fun he'd had seeing all the animals in the morning. How great it felt when his mum and David both said they were proud of him. Then the idea of making Lucky a hedgehog house was really exciting. He felt sure that he would see her again. Unfortunately, it had all gone wrong again! Perhaps David was right after all, maybe Lucky wasn't so lucky after all.

Chapter 30

William Pays The Price

Morning, Sunday November 5th

Early next morning, William and his stepdad went to check on the damage that the oil and paint cans had done to the car. David reversed out of the garage as William stood aside. The oil had left sticky green streaks down the paintwork and there were broad smears across the window and door where William had smudged it as he squeezed through the gap to free himself.

William waited anxiously as David prowled around the car peering closely at the paintwork and eventually he stood up. "You're lucky, I can't see any dents or deep scratches," David said sternly. "Those little ones should polish out with some elbow grease;

I'll show you how to clean it up properly and then you can get on with it."

"Okay," said William cheerfully. He was relieved that David seemed to be in a better mood this morning. He had feared that today was going to be horrible. However, his relief was short-lived. "Oh no, just look at that," David exclaimed loudly, pointing at the oil-smudged tyre tracks marking the garage floor.

"That's going to need some sand on it, or it will trail everywhere," he added angrily.

William looked at the mess in dismay; things were going wrong again even before he had started.

"Right, go and ask your mum for a bucket of warm water. Don't just stand there, move lad, there's work to be done," David said sharply, "and I'll go and get some sand from the shed."

Armed with a bucket, a sponge, car wash solution, and a chamois leather, William spent the rest of Sunday morning washing and polishing the car. David kept coming out to check on how he was doing. He even made him do some parts again if he thought they looked the slightest bit streaky.

Just when William thought he'd finished, David brought out the old vacuum cleaner and showed William how to clean the floor carpet and mats!

Suddenly, as he was vacuuming under the front passenger seat, the cleaner stopped working. *Oh no, please don't say it's broken, David will blame me again,* he thought as he backed out of the car. When he turned around, his mum was standing by the plug socket, smiling at him. She was holding a mug and a plate.

"I thought you might fancy some hot chocolate and some biscuits," she said.

"Oh, thanks Mum, it's tiring work all this cleaning and polishing."

"Tell me something I don't know," she said laughing. "Clearing up after you is a full-time job; perhaps you could try not to leave your clothes in a heap for the 'clothes fairy' to tidy up after you."

William loved it whenever his mum was smiling and teasing him. "Okay, I'll try to remember to tidy my things away, if you'll keep making hot chocolate for me. Do we have a deal?"

She tried to look as if she was cross with him, but her eyes were twinkling and the smile was still there when she said in a deep voice like David's, "I don't think you are in any position to be making deals my lad," which made them both laugh. Whilst William munched on a biscuit she added, "At least the trousers aren't ruined, I managed to get that oil out of them."

Relieved, William replied, "Thanks Mum, I'm really sorry about what happened. Is David still really mad at me?"

"Well, he's still annoyed, but he'll get over it, particularly as you've made such a good job of cleaning the car. There isn't much left to do is there? Why don't you ask him to help you make that feeding station? I'm sure he wouldn't mind."

"You must be joking, last night he said he wished I'd never set eyes on Lucky."

"I know, but that was last night, he's had time to cool off now. Just tell him how sorry you are and then ask him nicely," she suggested, putting her arm around William's shoulder...

Later that afternoon, William finally finished the car. He was sure it had never looked so clean and shiny, although he doubted if David would agree.

"I have to say you've done an excellent job, William, I'm impressed. I will give you some extra pocket money if you clean it like that every time."

Chapter 31

A Fresh Start

A little later that afternoon, Sunday November 5th

William was really surprised that David seemed so pleased with him. He took a breath and then said, "I am really sorry for making a mess of it and all the trouble I caused."

"Well let's forget it shall we? Anyway, your mum said I should say sorry for what I said about Lucky. So, I'm sorry William, I shouldn't have said that."

William couldn't believe what David had just said. His mum had worked her magic again! Spotting a golden opportunity, William asked, "You know the hedgehog house and feeding station that Mr Wilson suggested I make? I was wondering if you would help me to make them please?"

"I think that's probably a very good idea; after all, we don't want any more disasters do we?"

"I've looked at some websites that will show us how to do it properly," William said.

"Great, but we'll need to get a move on though, it will be dark soon," replied David, putting an arm on William's shoulder. "Don't forget we've got to get ready for tea at the Bedis'".

Within minutes, William had downloaded the plans from the 'British Hedgehog Preservation Society' website, and together they got to work. William was surprised how much he enjoyed working with David and in no time his plastic box had been transformed into a new hedgehog house with a much neater entrance hole. Perfect for Lucky and her 'big sleep' (hibernation).

Back in the garden, William and David considered where would be the best place to put the hedgehog house. They decided it would be against the fence, under some shrubs. David set to digging out the weeds and grass to create an earth floor whilst William collected as many branches and leaves as he could.

"The instructions suggest that the entrance to the house needs to be positioned out of the cold winds," said David, carefully placing it into position. Then together, he and William covered it with soil, clumps of turf, sticks and leaves to make it look like a natural den.

"Do you really think Lucky will find it?" William

asked, as he put the last of the leaves and branches around the side of the house.

"Well, we've done our best," David replied, "Now for the feeding station. You go and fetch four bricks from the pile behind the garage." William eagerly ran off down the path towards the house; he still couldn't believe David was being so nice. Meanwhile, David disappeared around the back of the shed, returning after a few minutes, staggering with the weight of the heavy concrete slab.

"Now, if you form the corners of the feeding station with those bricks I can lay this slab on top of them," David said, "don't hang about lad, this slab is heavy."

"Brill," said William, "that will allow Lucky to get at the mealworms and stop the birds and cats getting at them."

When they were satisfied that the job was finished, David stood up, massaging his back. "There's nothing more we can do now except put some food under there and keep our fingers crossed," he said.

William squatted down by the slab and spooned some of the chicken-flavoured cat food into the bowl and placed it under the slab. He sprinkled a handful of mealworms close to the entrance of the hedgehog house. William hadn't enjoyed himself this much in ages. This was definitely the best time he'd ever had with David.

"Thanks for helping me. I could never have done it on my own."

"Goodness, look at the time. We'd better get a

move on; we are due at the Bedis' for dinner at seven o'clock and it would be rude to be late. Now pick up some of these tools and I'll carry the rest."

Just then a firework rocketed up into the sky and exploded into hundreds of silver stars.

Chapter 32

It's A Nightmare

Sunday Evening, November 5th

'*I am really lucky to have found such a safe, cosy nest for my big sleep. Good night William, good night world, I'll see you in the spring,*' I thought as my eyes began to close. Everything was very still and quiet and soon I was back into my deep sleep….

I began having a strange dream. I had gone back in time. I was with my mother, my two brothers and sister Hetty. In my dream, our mum was warning all of us to be very careful as we prepared to cross the black stone road. She told us, in a very serious tone, that we must only cross it when it was dark and quiet. If ever we could hear a machine in the distance, or see moving lights, we must wait in the grass. She became very sad as she told us about the time her sister had been crushed by a machine when she had been dawdling as she crossed a busy road. We stared

144

at her with our eyes wide open in horror. My body shivered at the thought. She told us all to be quiet as she listened intently, and then looking around, she said:

"Go on, go now, whilst it's safe, now run along, be quick and don't stop or look back, like my sister did. I'll follow on behind you."

The four of us set off, running for our lives, looking straight ahead, not daring to pause for an instant. When we reached the other side of the road we turned around to look for mum, but she was nowhere to be seen. She had disappeared.

We began calling her, we even used our alarm squeals but there was no reply.

Hetty, our bossy sister, said in a tone which said don't argue, "Now you lot, stay here, don't go wandering off, I'll go back and find her." The rest of us huddled together and waited. Spike began crying, we were all very frightened.

"What if she's gone? What if we never see her again?" muttered Bugsy, so named because he always found the tastiest grubs.

"Now stop it, I'm sure mum wouldn't just leave us," I replied.

When Hetty eventually returned, she was extremely upset; it was as if she'd seen a ghost.

"I'm sorry, there's no sign of her. I tried to follow her scent the way she taught us to, but it was no use. I lost it when I came to the hard path that the machines use by their houses. I don't understand. Where has she gone?"

Spike was weeping now, and taking great heaving sobs between words he stammered, "b... but she... never even said g g... goodbye..."

I called out "Mum, where are you?"

I woke up, my heart was racing and I didn't know where I was. Slowly, I realised that it had been a terrible nightmare. I was snuggled down in my bed of leaves in my cosy den.

We never did see our mother again. Shortly afterwards, we all went our separate ways. I have not seen Hetty, Spike or Bugsy since. I felt terribly sad and lonely. At least the nest felt warm and dry. Hetty was smart and brave. I wondered if she was nearby, perhaps in a nest like this. What about little Spike? He was always the timid one, always the last to leave our nest to hunt for food. He stayed close to mum all the time and always did as he was told. Bugsy was always the first to go hunting at night; he'd come back and say he'd already eaten slugs, spiders and a juicy worm before the rest of us had even dared to go out. My eyes began to sting with tears so I squeezed them shut and burrowed deep down into my cosy bed.

"I hope you are all safe and doing okay?" I whispered, "it would be great to see you all again."

Chapter 33

A Night To Remember

Early evening, Sunday November 5th

Meanwhile, David stopped the car outside the Bedis'
home. "Well, it's ten past seven, this is the right
address, now be polite and don't let us down, son,"
he said, giving William a warning look.

"Remember, only take a little food onto your plate
as you might not like it at first; you can then leave it
and try something else," suggested his mum.

"I love Asian food," said David as he pressed the
doorbell.

They could hear voices behind the door and
through the stained glass panels saw people moving
about. It was opened by a tall, slim man with a thick
black beard and smiling eyes; William knew it was

Parveen's dad because she had told him her father wore a turban on his head, as a symbol of the Sikh religion.

"Welcome, welcome, come on in, you are most welcome, my name is Mohan and this is my wife Sunitta," he said.

As they entered the hallway, Mr Bedi shook William's hand and said, "Ah, you must be William. You are a very brave young man, we are truly grateful to you. Goodness me, look at your eye, it must have been very painful."

William smiled, he felt very embarrassed receiving such praise. Standing behind Mr Bedi, William could see Parveen's mum. She had long shiny black hair, just like Parveen's. She was wearing a sparkly blue top over her black trousers. She smiled as she shook his hand, causing her gold bracelets to tinkle together, "Hello, William, it is lovely to meet you."

Just then Parveen came skipping down the stairs. William thought how different she looked in a T-shirt with jeans and trainers.

"Hello William, hello Mr and Mrs Harrison," she said politely.

"May I introduce my troublesome daughter, Parveen. If you have room in your car and need a daughter please feel free to take her home with you," Mr Bedi teased, and everyone laughed. Turning to David, he continued, "I believe you've met our other daughter, Narinder. She is staying with her auntie tonight. I think she was a bit worried about having her deputy head teacher coming to her house."

"That's a shame, but tell her that she needn't have worried as school is school and home is completely separate; but I will tell you though that she's a lovely girl, she's doing really well and we have high hopes for her," David said.

Moments later, after coats had been removed, everyone was seated around the table. Mrs Bedi and Parveen began bringing in various bowls of food that looked and smelled completely different to anything William had ever seen or eaten before.

Parveen's mum served them all and she explained to William that he should pick up the samosa with his fingers. Remembering what his mum had said, William took a tentative bite. Everyone went quiet and seemed to be watching him as he slowly chewed the food. They were waiting to see if he liked the spicy taste. Suddenly, the flavours seemed to make his tongue tingle. "This is delicious," he said, taking another bigger mouthful. Everyone relaxed and got on with enjoying the feast.

William was amazed as dish after dish of food was brought to the table. As the meal eventually came to a close, Parveen's brother, Manjit, appeared for the first time. He was wrapped up in a warm hat and coat. He reached across the table and picked up one of the delicious sweets that William had particularly enjoyed.

"Everything's ready dad; better get on with it though as there's a massive storm coming," he said.

"Good, good, now everybody let's go over to the patio window. You do like fireworks don't you William?" said Mr Bedi.

"Oh wow, I love fireworks," replied William excitedly.

"Well that's a good job; now make sure you can all see," Mr Bedi said, ushering William into the best position.

William could see that Manjit was back outside in the garden, his torchlight aimed at a pile of bricks that looked like a chimney on the lawn. He bent down and lit a fuse. It burst into life, spitting bright sparks. Suddenly, 'WHOOSH' and a brilliant white star flew up into the night sky. 'BOOM' there was a loud explosion, followed by a burst of glittering silver stars which drifted down on the slight breeze. "Wow," gasped William, 'WHOOSH' another, then another and so it went on. They watched, mouths gaping in awe, each saying things like, "Oh wow", "beautiful", "awesome", "brilliant", "spectacular" and "amazing" as the dazzling fireworks whistled, crackled, whizzed and banged sending their purple, gold and green stars into the sky. Rockets went up with a 'SWOOSH' before bursting into a rainbow of colours. As the last firework died down and thick grey smoke swirled around the garden, everyone began clapping Manjit for lighting them.

Just then, a dazzling flash of lightning lit up the garden followed almost immediately by a booming rumble of thunder that made the windows rattle. Mr Bedi invited everyone to return to the dining table. He asked if anyone would like tea or coffee. William's mum replied saying, "Thank you, but we'd better not, it's getting late and it is a school day tomorrow so we'd better make a move." She turned to Parveen's mum. "It's been a lovely evening. Sunitta, I'd love to know how you made those wonderful samosas; they were delicious. You must all come over to us before Christmas. I'll call you to fix a date."

William said, "That was the best fireworks ever," and he meant it.

"You're right son, that was a truly splendid show Mohan, and Manjit you did a great job out there. Thank you so much and thank you, Sunitta, for the lovely food, it was truly a feast," said David.

After Mr Bedi had handed them all their coats, they gathered in the hallway and either shook hands or exchanged hugs. Another dazzling flash of lightning was immediately following by a long, menacing growl of thunder as they opened the front door. Then the first large raindrops began to fall. David clicked his key ring and the car doors unlocked. They rushed to get in and fasten their seatbelts as the rain turned into a torrential downpour. After a final wave to the family huddled in the doorway, David switched the windscreen wipers on to full speed. 'Swish, slosh, swish, slosh, swish, slosh,' they went as they struggled to cope with the downpour.

"Typical," he moaned, "Can you believe this Margaret? What a change. Last night was really cold and frosty and now look at it and the car was really clean."

"Oh it doesn't matter, David, we've had a lovely evening haven't we?" replied William's mum. The wipers continued their rhythmical swish, slosh, swish, slosh as she continued, "Those fireworks must have cost a fortune. They were brilliant, weren't they son?"

"They were amazing," said William from the back seat.

David said, "Weren't we lucky with the weather? I bet it's ruined that big display the Taylors were planning in their field at the back of our orchard."

"Yes, it's a shame, I bet everyone has got soaked and gone home," said William's mum.

Just as they turned into their driveway the rain stopped. David switched off the wipers, and said, "Would you believe it?"

William's mum took charge. "Right William, straight up to bed for you. I'll bring you a hot chocolate, same for you David?"

"That would be great love, I'll just put the car away," said David, unlocking the back door to let William and his mum into the house.

Chapter 34

I Know I'm Going To Die

Night-time, Sunday November 5th

Back in my den in the meadow beyond the orchard, two very loud noises startled me. The bangs were followed by terrible shrieking whistles that set my heart racing. *Oh no, there must be monsters about,* I thought, *I wonder if they know I'm here?* I could hear human voices close by. Were those boys coming back to find me? My sensitive nose started to twitch, what was that strange smell?

'SWOOSH!' Suddenly I could see flames licking at the branches above me. Thick black smoke began drifting and swirling around in between the gaps in the timbers. It stung my eyes and made my throat burn as I gasped for breath. Leaves shrivelled up and popped before bursting into flames. I was trapped. *I needed to get out of there somehow, but how?* The wooden boards were blocking my escape. Just above me the flames were now licking around the edges of the wooden pieces. The dry leaves in my bed began to smoke. I tried gulping in some air but the heat made my chest hurt. I could see a tiny gap between two boards so I tried to squeeze between them but it was too narrow. I was stuck, I couldn't move forwards or backwards. I was panicking. I started digging as fast as I could. My powerful claws ripping and tearing at the soft turf but it was no use, I was stuck fast. I realised that I couldn't move. I was going to burn to death!

Above me a board creaked and made a loud snapping sound. Sparks flew all around as a branch crashed down onto my back. I could smell my spines burning. I squealed in pain. I was in agony. I was on fire. A voice in my head said, '*Dig, Lucky, dig for your life!*' The gap slowly widened as I continued clawing at the soil. My feet were bleeding now as they ripped at the soil…

At last, I could feel a draft of cool night air. '*Come on Lucky, keep going,*' the voice said. More branches fell around me. My bedding suddenly burst into flames filling my den with thick, black, choking smoke. The heat was unbearable. My lungs felt like they were on fire. The voice in my head kept saying, '*Come on, Lucky, don't give up now.*' I tried one final push, straining with all my might. '*Pushhhh!*'

Like a cork out of a bottle I managed to pop through the tiny gap! I tried to run away from the flames but I had no energy left, I just collapsed. The damp grass felt soothing and cool against my belly and I took several deep gulps of cool air. I was so tired I just wanted to close my eyes and sleep.

There was another very loud bang and the heat from the fire continued scorching me. *I must get away from here somehow.* There were no bushes nearby to shelter under, only some thistles and large dock leaves. I dragged myself forward and hid. Stabbing pains shot down my back each time I moved.

'Whoosh', a bright star soared up into the inky black sky. 'Wheeee, wheeee, wheeee', another one shrieked. Not monsters after all. I could see the shadowy shapes of humans standing on the far side of the fire.

I could see their faces glowing brightly in the flickering firelight. I knew I must move away before they saw me. I was exhausted, too weak to move, there was nothing I could do but wait to die...

Then a flash of bright light split the dark night followed immediately by a low rumble in the sky which became louder and louder. Huge raindrops suddenly poured down. They hissed and steamed as they landed on the fire and on my back. I could hear the humans screaming as they ran away, some of them into their noisy machines.

The torrential rain felt cool and soothing on my scorched back. I was in agony and too weak to move. I lay still and licked my aching paws and tasted my own blood. The voice inside my head spoke again, *'Go to William, Lucky.'* I realised then that William was my only chance. Somehow, I had to get to him. He would know what to do. Only he could save me.

If I stayed here, I would certainly die. I summoned up the last remaining strength in my aching body and began to crawl towards the orchard... step by agonising step...

Chapter 35

Being Brave

Later that night, Sunday November 5th

William got changed into his pyjamas before going into the bathroom and brushing his teeth. Back in his bedroom he walked across to the window to close the curtains. He looked out into the darkness and he could see the orange glow and small flames flickering from the bonfire in the meadow beyond the orchard. He could make out some shadowy figures silhouetted against the flames. They kept darting forwards towards the fire and then retreating back into the darkness. They appeared to be trying to do something to the fire. *What are they up to?* he thought.

Suddenly, a bright tongue of flame leapt out of the fire and engulfed one of the figures! William watched in horror as the person staggered backwards, their arms flailing as if they were being attacked by a swarm of bees. The victim fell backwards onto the ground highlighted by the glow from the flames. Flames licked at his clothing, like a hungry dragon preparing to feed. Two shadowy figures ran across to the victim and they appeared to be trying to put out the flames and then one of them picked something up and threw it onto the fire. The figures then disappeared into the darkness.

William dashed for the stairs, shouting, "Mum, Dad! Quick! Somebody's on fire in the meadow."

He raced through the kitchen, pulled his wellingtons on, grabbed his coat and ran outside. William sprinted down the garden, flinging open the gate into the orchard. He ran as fast he could, his coat billowing behind him. He slowed only to scramble through the hedge. Thorns scratched at his hands and face as he pushed his way through the small gap. It was the same gap the boys had used to get into the orchard when they had been stealing apples.

He got down onto his hands and knees and crawled under the wire fence into the meadow. He heard his coat tear as he rushed to get to his feet. The grass was soaking wet and now his pyjamas were too. A short distance ahead, he could see the fire dying back down, casting an eerie light over the area.

"Help me!" a voice groaned out from the darkness before erupting into a bout of coughing. "Somebody please help me."

William ran in the direction of the voice, calling out

as he ran, "Hold on, I'm coming." He rushed up to the figure lying on the ground. He could hear the person sobbing as he knelt down beside him. William could see it was a young boy about his own age. His clothes were scorched and blackened. In the flickering light William could see the skin on his hands was red and blistered. William quickly stripped off his coat and wrapped it around the boys' shoulders. As he turned the boy over he recognised his face. "It's you!" he exclaimed. "Let me put this over you. It will keep you warm."

'Boom!' Flames suddenly leapt skywards as a massive explosion sent sparks and burning embers shooting up into the air. The fire had exploded back into life. William leaned over the boy to shield him as the flaming embers rained down around them.

David called out from the other side of the hedge in the orchard, "William, are you injured? Where are you?"

"Over here Dad, I'm okay. It's Tommy Smithers, he's badly burned."

"Don't worry, just hang on, we've already called 999, help is coming, are you okay?"

"Yes, Dad, but we're freezing out here."

"Hang on, I'm going to the garage, I need to widen this gap for the paramedics. I'll get some blankets for you both."

There was a brief silence and then David shouted out again, "Margaret! Margaret! Can you get some rugs or blankets please… quickly now." With that he was gone and William was left with Tommy in the darkness…

The fire was dying down again and he could see the ashes glowing and fading like a faint pulse as the breeze blew over them. William looked back towards the house and noticed that lights had gone on upstairs in a number of the houses in the road.

"Where is Mum with those blankets?" he muttered, and then his teeth began chattering so much that he couldn't stop them. Tommy too was shivering, his whole body trembling; it was as if he was being given an electric shock.

William spotted the beam from the torchlight swinging as his stepdad ran through the orchard. "I'm coming, William," he shouted, and moments later added, "now, grab these duvets and wrap yourselves in them whilst I cut the fence wire and open up this gap."

Sirens wailed in the distance racing against time.

William ran back to Tommy. "Come on Tommy, we need to keep warm, let me put this around you."

William noticed that it was the duvet off his bed, as he carefully rolled Tommy over trying not to hurt him. His fingers were tingling with the cold as he struggled to pull the edge of the duvet around Tommy's chest. Tommy was groaning, but he didn't speak or open his eyes, his whole body was shaking so much. William draped the other duvet around himself. It felt as if he was sitting in an ice cold bath. David ran over to them and shone the torch in Tommy's face. It was blackened with soot but at least there were no signs of burns. Tommy screwed his eyes tight shut against the light and groaned again. When the light shone on his right arm, however, it was obvious that it was seriously burned. The skin was badly blistered and there were patches of red, angry skin across Tommy's wrist and knuckles.

"Your mum's waiting for the ambulance and fire brigade; they shouldn't be long now but they said it is their busiest night of the year!" David said to William.

The sirens sounded louder and louder and then stopped. William heard the fire engine's air brakes make a loud hissing sound as they pulled up: 'Pweshsh' He could see the blue lights flashing against the walls of the neighbours' houses.

David shone his torch on the gap he'd made in the hedge to guide the paramedics in their green overalls to where William and Tommy were. Soon they were squatting down on either side of Tommy. The woman shone a bright torch into Tommy's face, whilst holding his wrist. Tommy screwed up his eyes and groaned.

"Okay young man, my name's Sharon, can you talk to me? What's your name son?" There was no reply.

William said, "His name is Tommy Smithers, he goes to my school."

"Okay, Tommy, let's take a look shall we?" She turned to her partner and said, "Phil, we need to get some oxygen and adrenalin into him. Don't want him to get any worse. I'll put a thermal blanket on him."

"Gotcha Sharon, I'll see if those boys from the brigade can give us a hand with the stretcher."

A tall fireman joined them. "Looks like the fire is almost out, but we'll need to damp it down to make sure. It's the third call tonight to put bonfires out. Are these two scallywags going to be okay?" he said looking in William's direction.

David bristled at the suggestion that William was involved in any way.

"Excuse me, officer, but it was my son William here who spotted that this lad was messing around up here," he said indignantly. "He dashed out in his pyjamas to save him when he saw him on fire, look!" he added, removing the blanket over William's legs to reveal his 'Superman' pyjamas.

"Okay sir. However, the police will need to talk to him tomorrow; it's standard procedure just to find out exactly what happened here." He glanced towards Tommy who now had an oxygen mask covering his face and a special burns wrapping on his right hand and arm. Another fireman approached them carrying a scorched petrol can. "I've found this; it looks like the kids were trying to get the fire going again. They were being really stupid," he said.

"He was really lucky that this young man spotted him," said Sharon, who then turned to her colleague. "Phil, call Camford Hospital and tell them we've got a young male coming in. He'll need a bed for the night. Then see if we can get hold of his parents; I'm going to check on this young man. Then we'll load young Tommy up and get on our way."

William's mum came running towards the group.

"Oh son, thank God you're safe," she said, wrapping him up into her arms in a bear hug.

"He isn't injured is he?" she said anxiously as she turned towards the paramedic.

"No madam," she replied, "I'm just going to check him over and then treat those scratches; we don't want them becoming infected, then he's all yours."

William's mum let go of him and allowed the paramedic to check William over. She shone a light into his eyes and said, "Blimey, that's quite a black eye you've got, who did that to you William?"

"It was him," replied William, pointing at Tommy. "We had a fight at school."

Sharon took hold of William's wrist and checked his pulse and nodded.

"Right then, time to be brave again young man as this is going to sting a bit," and she continued treating the deepest of William's scratches.

One of the fire crew came towards them out of the darkness, his helmet lamp shining brightly. He was holding something very carefully in his thick gloves.

"Looks like this little chap must have been trapped in the bonfire when it was lit. Don't suppose you can do anything for the poor thing can you?"

"Here let me see," said Sharon. "Can you shine your head lamp onto it?" The fireman bent his head down and the powerful beam of light illuminated the creature cradled within his thick gloves. "Blimey, it's a hedgehog. It's still alive, but only just; look at those spines on its back, what a mess!" she said.

"It's so sad, the poor thing is in a really bad way, probably best if we put it out of its misery?" suggested the fireman.

William scrambled to his feet saying, "Let me see, let me see." He looked at the bundle in the fireman's hands and said immediately, "It's Lucky, it's Lucky," he said excitedly, "see her jaw is crooked, it's Lucky. You can't let her die. You must do something!"

"Lucky! Who's Lucky?" asked Sharon.

David interrupted, "It's a long story, but William here rescued her when some lads were pelting her with stones. That is how her jaw got broken," he added, "in fact, William saved her life."

"You've got to do something," pleaded William, "you can't let her die. Tell them Dad. Please Dad, don't let her die," he begged, and large wet tears began running down his cheeks.

Sharon looked across to her colleague, Phil, who was busy fastening the straps around Tommy on the stretcher. "What do you think?"

"Look, much as I would like to help, we've got to get this lad into hospital. We cannot waste time attempting to save a dying hedgehog, Sharon."

He turned towards William and said, "I'm very sorry son."

"Listen," said the fireman. "I've got an idea. If a couple of the lads carry the stretcher into the ambulance with you Phil, Sharon here can then spend a few minutes trying to help this little chap. What do you think?" Phil and Sharon looked at each other and shrugged.

Phil said, "Okay, after what you've done tonight, the least we can do is try and give Lucky a chance. Only two minutes mind, we need to get that lad to hospital."

"Great, let's do this," said the fireman before calling out to his colleagues who were finishing off dousing the bonfire. "Winston, Raffa, come here quickly lads; we've got a stretcher to move." The two firemen switched off the hose straight away and jogged over to the group.

Phil said, "Thanks lads, you know how this works? Nice and level and as quickly as we can; he's very cold and we don't want him to suffer hypothermia."

"Speaking of cold, we're freezing out here, let's get back inside and get warm," said David as he put his arm around William's shoulder.

"We all need a warm drink too, don't we? I'll make us all that hot chocolate now," suggested William's mum.

The group hurried through the orchard, towards the house, carefully stepping over the thick fire hoses that snaked up their driveway, on their way to the meadow. William could see the ambulance and fire engine through the living room window, their lights still blinking and bouncing off the walls of the houses. A few neighbours were standing around looking on and trying to find out what had happened.

In the kitchen, William's mum quickly spread some towels on the table and the fireman gently placed Lucky in the middle. Sharon was rummaging in her bag. She took out another oxygen mask, wiped it with a disinfectant wipe before placing it over Lucky's head. She adjusted the valve on the cylinder to minimum and switched it on.

"I'm going to treat Lucky like a premature, new born baby," she said. "Poor little thing will have inhaled smoke and we need to flush it out very gently with oxygen."

After a few moments she turned to William. "Now William, if you can hold that tube just there, then I can have a look at these burns," she said, before gently examining the wound across her back. It was raw and much of the flesh was blistered, many of the spines had melted and others were blackened and scorched.

"She is going to be get better, isn't she?" asked William anxiously.

"I won't lie to you, I'm no vet but it's going to be touch and go," Sharon replied, a grim expression on her face. "She's obviously a tough little thing, given what she's been through."

"It was as if she was making for the orchard," said the fireman, "perhaps she was trying to get to you."

Sharon, the paramedic, sprayed Lucky's wounds with a special burns treatment. "This artificial skin is wonderful stuff. It will keep the fluid in and reduce the risk of shock and infection. If she pulls through tonight she has a chance. She'll need to see a vet first thing tomorrow to get some fluids, special animal antibiotics and mineral supplements."

At that moment William's mum announced, "Hot

drinks are ready, help yourselves to biscuits. William, here's your chocolate," passing him a mug.

He took it in both hands without taking his eyes off Sharon as she worked on Lucky.

"What do you say, son?" reminded David.

"Sorry Dad," William said quickly, "thanks Mum, its lovely."

"Nearly done," said Sharon, bending down and removing a syringe from her bag. "I'm going to inject her with some water and glucose. It will give her a start but if she wakes up someone will need to give her some more, just a few drops onto her lips every hour or so."

Sharon's colleague Phil entered the already very crowded kitchen. "Come on Sharon, we have to be going. I've made the lad as comfortable as possible, and he's on the drip. The police have traced his parents, they put a call out, and they are going to meet us at the hospital; so how are you doing?"

"All done," said Sharon removing the oxygen mask. "I've done the best I can. I've a feeling it's going to be a long night for Lucky; good luck everyone," and then she picked up her bag and helped herself to two chocolate biscuits as she walked out.

"Thank you for all you've done, both for William and Tommy and not forgetting Lucky. We are so grateful to you," David said following them to the door.

Chapter 36

It's Going To Be A Long Night

Very late on Sunday November 5th

The tall fireman who had found Lucky was rubbing his chin thoughtfully.

"I've got an idea that I think might work, but I'll need to clear it with my boss though. I'll be back in a minute!"

It suddenly went a lot quieter in the kitchen as William munched on a biscuit and sipped his drink, never once taking his eyes off Lucky.

"Now son, go and get out of those soaking pyjamas straight away. I'll run the water for a hot bath and put some clothes ready for you on your bed."

"What about Lucky Mum, she needs me?" William said, his voice trembling.

"Don't worry, Lucky is resting now. David and I will keep an eye on her until you come back down," she replied.

William bent down towards his helpless little friend and whispered, "Hang on Lucky, don't give up, I'll look after you, I promise; please don't die."

He turned and ran up the stairs. He stripped off his damp pyjamas and left them in a pile and soon was soaking in the warm bath. It felt lovely after being so cold. He would really have liked to have a long soak but he was desperate to get back to Lucky.

His mum guessed that he wouldn't stay in the bath for long so she spoke to him through the bathroom door. "You need to get properly warmed through William. I don't want you being ill as well. You'll have to stay in there for at least ten minutes. If you don't, David and I will send you straight to bed and you won't be able to look after Lucky, do you hear me?"

William was surprised how firm his mum sounded and he knew better than to argue. "Okay Mum," he replied reluctantly.

After his bath, William dressed in his woolly jumper and tracksuit bottoms that his mum had put ready. As he was giving his thick hair a quick rub with the towel, the clock downstairs began to chime; it was half past eleven. He dashed downstairs but he couldn't believe the sight that greeted him in the kitchen.

Chapter 37

We Need A Miracle

Just before midnight, Sunday November 5th

David was holding the fireman's yellow helmet whilst the fireman was carefully lowering Lucky into it. He was placing Lucky onto a bed made up of tea towels.

"What are you doing?" asked William anxiously.

David replied, "Graham here," he said nodding towards the fireman, "worked out that we could get more oxygen into Lucky if we used the breathing apparatus the firemen use when they enter a smoke-filled room. He got special permission off his station commander. We're just going to use some tape on the visor to keep the oxygen inside the helmet."

"Right that's it," said Graham as he finished with the tape. "I'd better be off. The lads will wonder where I've got to; they should be almost finished up by now."

Suddenly, the back door opened and Winston and Raffa, the two firemen who had carried the stretcher, entered the room. They were both smiling and the one William remembered as Raffa took out his phone and began taking photos of Lucky in her improvised 'oxygen tent'.

"They won't believe this back at the station, and it'll go viral on the internet," he said.

They stayed for a few more minutes to have a drink and some biscuits before they too were on their way. The huge red engine clattered and then roared into life with a cloud of blue exhaust smoke. Winston waved through the driver's door window as they pulled away.

David returned to the kitchen. "What a night that was," he said, glancing at the helmet. "Well it's off to bed now, it's nearly midnight!"

William couldn't believe what David had said. "Dad, I have to stay up, I will have to feed Lucky when she wakes up," he pleaded, looking at his mum for support.

"Please Mum; Lucky will die if we don't give her a feed every hour. You heard Sharon, didn't you?"

"Yes I did son, and I know how much this means to you. I'll stay up with you as long as you promise to go to bed early tomorrow night and catch up," she said stroking his hair.

"Well, it looks like we're all staying up. I'll go and fetch the duvet off our bed and the sleeping bags from the spare room, at least we'll be snug," said David dimming the lights down…

For the next two hours they kept checking on Lucky but there was no change, she didn't move at all. William sat by the table; he felt so tired and he wanted to put his head down, close his eyes and go to sleep. Something inside though was telling him that if he went to sleep, Lucky would never wake up. The thought brought more tears to his eyes. He looked across at his mum and David. They were both snoozing on the sofa.

"Looks like it's just you and me now," whispered William. "Come on Lucky, wake up. Please…"

As William stared through the helmet's visor he thought he saw Lucky's leg twitch. "Are you dreaming Lucky?" he spoke aloud, "or am I dreaming?" No there it was again, Lucky's leg definitely moved again. "Come on Lucky don't give up now." After another twitch, William called out excitedly, "Dad, Mum put the lights on, come and look; I think she's waking up. Come on Lucky I'm here for you……"

Chapter 38

Have I Died Or Am I Dreaming?

Before dawn, Monday November 6th

I must be dreaming. I am running, the monster with the big teeth is chasing me. My chest is stinging and my back feels like it's on fire. It really hurts as I move. I can see smoke swirling around me, my head is pounding and I feel really thirsty. I can hear someone calling me, "Come on Lucky wake up…Come on Lucky, I'm here for you," the voice kept saying. As I opened my eyes, there was a bright light dazzling me… I could just make out William's face smiling at me…

FURTHER INFORMATION AND USEFUL CONTACTS

*Here you can find out more about the lives of our
spiky friends below:*

Hedgehog numbers in the UK have fallen
dramatically in recent years from an estimated 36
million in the 1950s down to around just 1 million
now. If we don't create suitable habitat for them and
other wildlife in our towns and cities we risk losing
them forever.

TYPICAL HEDGEHOG ACTIVITY
MONTH BY MONTH

Month	Activity
January	Hibernating
February	Hibernating but their fat reserves will be very low.
March	Some hogs awake, especially in mild winters.
April	Now active; they need to build up their body weight again.
May	Males seek mates. Females (hopefully) become pregnant.

June	Typically babies born this month. They are born blind and remain in the nest.
July	Mother and babies leave nest together.
August	Young leave their nest and become independent. If you are lucky enough to have hedgehogs in your garden, you can help by leaving cat meat (not fish varieties) and water out for them. **Never give hedgehogs milk! They are lactose intolerant.**
September	Late litters may produce autumn orphans unable to cope with winter weather so will need to be over-wintered by carers or taken to a local 'Rescue Centre'.
October	Winter nests are built and hogs build up their fat reserves.
November	Most hogs will now begin to hibernate, although in mild winters some hogs do not hibernate but they will need help with food and unfrozen water left for them.
December	Mostly hibernating, some may occasionally wake for food.

Also check out the following reference pages for more fun information about hedgehogs and how you can help them.

WHAT TO DO IF YOU FIND A HEDGEHOG

Hedgehogs are nocturnal animals; this means they should be asleep during the daytime. They usually only come out at night to hunt for food and to mate. Therefore, if you see a hedgehog during the daytime they are possibly in trouble.

Mothers do occasionally leave the nest to feed

and get a rest from the litter. This will most likely occur between April and September. If the hedgehog appears to be fit and well, it is best to leave it alone.

HOWEVER

Any of the situations listed below could mean that the hedgehog is in trouble and could need emergency care:

- If the hedgehog is squealing or screaming.
- If the hedgehog is injured or bleeding.
- If it is gasping for breath.
- If it is caught up in netting or other litter.
- If the hedgehog looks wobbly on its feet.
- If it is covered in flies or maggots.
- If it appears to be having a fit or seizure.
- If it appears to be hyperactive.
- If it appears to be sleeping or sunbathing during the day.

Call your local Hedgehog Rescue or vets for advice.

WHAT TO DO IN AN EMERGENCY

Pick up the hedgehog gently using an old towel or thick gardening gloves because their spines are very sharp.

Line a high-sided box (at least 20cm high) with newspaper so it cannot climb out.

Place the hedgehog inside the box and put a towel or blanket over it to keep it warm. Injured hedgehogs may be cold and could suffer from shock.

Offer a shallow dish of water

BUT DO NOT FEED IT UNTIL YOU HAVE BEEN GIVEN ADVICE.
REMEMBER… NEVER OFFER HEDGEHOGS BREAD OR MILK AS IT MAKES THEM VERY ILL!

WHY DO HEDGEHOGS HIBERNATE?

When the ground is frozen or covered in snow it would be almost impossible for a hedgehog to get enough beetles, worms, etc. to survive. Also during the cold days and nights it would lose so much heat and use up so much energy trying to keep warm and find food that it could not survive.

Therefore, when the hours of daylight get shorter and the air temperature falls, it triggers a hormonal (chemical reaction) change within the hedgehog which signals that it is time for it to hibernate.

When a hedgehog hibernates it finds a cosy nest of leaves and curls up into a very tight ball to conserve its body heat before it goes into a condition known as **'torpor'. Check out the 'super powers' of our amazing spiky friends.** In this state its heart rate will slow right down from 190 beats per minute to just 20. So imagine you had been racing around the athletics track and when you finish you are out of breath and your heart is racing at 200 beats per minute to pump oxygen to your muscles and brain. That is how fast a hedgehog heart is beating normally. It also slows its breathing rate right down too. If you are in a swimming pool and you try to hold your breath under water you are doing well if you can manage 45 seconds. Well, our spiky friends only breathe once every few minutes when they go into hibernation.

Another 'super power' it uses to survive is that it allows its core body temperature to drop down from 35 degrees centigrade down to 10 degrees. Most animals would not be able to survive such a drop in body temperature. It is this drop in temperature which helps it to live off its reserves of fat built up in the autumn.

Authors Questions and Answers

What do you hope your readers will take away with them when reading the book?

Firstly, I hope everyone who reads it really enjoys the story and can relate to the characters. William, like most children and young adults face difficulties and challenges as they try to make sense of their lives.

Also, I wanted to give children a glimpse into the nocturnal lives of Britain's most iconic animal and one whose very future is in serious doubt.

For parents and teachers I wanted the short chapter format written from the point of view of the two main characters to add pace, interest and 'stopping places' to facilitate discussions about the issues raised in the storyline.

What was the inspiration behind this book?

Luckily for me a number of factors all came together to write a book about animals and wildlife.

I grew up reading the adventures of Hal and Roger

Hunt, two characters created by Willard Price in series of books involving wildlife adventures. The first book to make me cry was, 'Tan a Wild Dog,' written by Thomas C. Hinkle. I thoroughly recommend it. Latterly the brilliant stories of Michael Morpurgo, Dick King-Smith and Gill Lewis are always a source of inspiration.

Then we were invited to release a very fat hedgehog that we named, 'Chubby,' into our garden. Chubby had been rescued and rehabilitated in a local hedgehog rescue. Thankfully he stuck around, visiting our hedgehog feeding stations most evenings which enabled me to get some lovely video footage. This inspired me to want to learn more about the nocturnal habits of these amazing animals.

My research lead me to the appalling discovery that hedgehog numbers are declining rapidly from an estimated 30 million in the 1950's down to just over 1 million in 1995 and declining further. (Source: Peoples Trust for Endangered Species, Hedgehog Street.) Hopefully this book and the talks I give on behalf of hedgehog rescue centres will help raise awareness of their plight.

William is not a typical hero. Why did you choose to create a main character facing so many challenges in his life?

I think that by giving William the sort of challenges faced by many children and young adults, it makes him more interesting as a character. I also think readers will be able to identify with many of the challenges he faces both at home and at school. It would be brilliant if parents and teachers could shape some discussions based upon the feelings and emotions generated by verbal bullying, bereavement, keeping ones temper under control, prejudice and discrimination to help children understand life's up and downs.

The author Robert A Brown
Can be contacted via Alexa Davis, Troubador Publishing Ltd
9 Priory Business Park, Kibworth, Leicester.
or via
robertabrownauthor@outlook.com

Facebook WilliamTheHedgehogBoy
Twitter #WilliamTheHedgehogBoy

CONTACTS TO HELP YOU TO FIND OUT MORE ABOUT HEDGEHOGS

British Hedgehog Preservation Society –
Hedgerow House, Dhustone, Ludlow, SY8 3PL:
Telephone 01584 890801
bhps@dhustone.fsbusiness.co.uk
or
www.britishhedgehogs.org.uk
They can also provide details of your local hedgehog
rescue centre.

People's Trust for Endangered Species:
www.ptes.org and enquiries@ptes.org
The People's Trust for Endangered Species website
also features
The Hedgehog Street web page.

Snuffles Hedgehog Rescue –
Four Oaks, Sutton Coldfield B74 4YB:
Telephone 07889770958
www.snuffles-rescue.com

Care, treatment and rehabilitation for sick, injured and orphaned hedgehogs

Tamworth and District Hedgehog & Bird Rescue-
31 Hayworth Close, Tamworth, B79 8ER
Telephone 01827 701219
carol.tyler2@ntlworld.com
Community focused hedgehog and wild bird rescue centre

Royal Society for the Protection of Birds – the RSPB:
www.rspb.org.uk is running a Give wildlife a home campaign packed with ideas about what you can do and how to get involved.

Tiggywinkles Wildlife Hospital
Aston Road, Haddenham, Aylesbury HP17 8AF
Telephone 01844 292292l
mail@tiggywinkles.org or www.tiggywinkles.org.uk
This is the world famous hospital caring for hedgehogs and many other wildlife species that have been seriously injured.

To find out more about Lucky and her spiky friends visit: Amazon, Google Playstore websites and major bookships including Foyles, Waterstones and W.H.Smith and your local library.

Some TOP TIPS for keeping our wonderful hedgehogs safe: NB: The tips below are taken from a range of sources and many of the websites listed earlier:-

- Every year many hedgehogs are seriously injured or killed by gardening equipment.
- ALWAYS check for hedgehogs carefully before STRIMMING, MOWING GRASS or DIGGING OVER COMPOST..
- DO NOT USE SLUG PELLETS or PESTICIDES as both hedgehogs and birds eat the slugs which have been poisoned and then die themselves.
- Create a ramp to allow hedgehogs to escape from ponds or pools. They can swim but often drown because they cannot get out.
- Create a hedgehog highway by making a gap about the size of a DVD COVER in garden fences so that hedgehogs can wander freely between gardens at night.
- Buy or make a feeding station and feed meat-based dog/cat food in jelly rather than gravy.
- ALWAYS ensure fresh water is available in shallow dishes/trays.

- Keep garden nets 0.5 metres above the ground so that hedgehogs don't get tangled up in it.
- Always check for hedgehogs before lighting bonfires, moving leaves or digging over compost.
- Dispose of drink cans and particularly ring pulls properly to avoid wildlife getting injured.

Lucky the Hedgehog Word Search

Reproduced with kind permission of Claire Hunt and the team at Snuffles.

N	O	C	T	U	R	N	A	L	S	U	B	J	V
F	I	T	O	N	E	Q	H	E	C	L	F	I	L
S	Z	J	W	Q	M	E	A	L	W	O	R	M	I
N	O	R	T	H	W	L	D	C	A	U	J	E	N
U	R	K	V	O	U	R	C	S	A	X	I	U	S
F	H	E	D	G	E	H	O	G	H	O	U	S	E
F	E	A	R	L	G	J	L	S	I	F	H	P	C
L	O	R	B	E	E	T	L	E	B	Z	K	I	T
E	D	T	I	T	G	O	A	L	E	E	A	N	L
S	A	H	N	M	G	J	Q	D	R	K	F	E	A
W	O	W	E	B	D	K	C	W	N	N	E	S	T
S	N	O	R	T	A	O	U	E	A	W	O	R	D
I	A	R	T	C	Z	U	R	R	T	G	R	O	S
R	H	M	A	M	M	A	L	T	E	A	E	I	O

Can you find these words?

hoglet	spines	nest curl
hibernate	beetle	mammal
snuffles	hedgehog house	nocturnal
snort		insect
earthworm	mealworm	

Good luck everyone!!
Lucky the Hedgehog- Fun Facts Quiz

1. How many of us hedgehogs do you think there are left in the Great Britain? Are there,
A) ABOUT 1 MILLION?
B) ABOUT 1000? or
C) ABOUT 20 million?

2. Can you think of any other British animals, birds or insects that come out at night to feed like us?

3. On average how many spines do you think we hedgehogs have? Is it,
A) 5-7000?
B) Less than 5000? or
C) OVER 9000?

4. How do we hedgehogs protect ourselves when attacked or frightened? Do we,
A) RUN AWAY AND HIDE?
B) FIGHT? or
C) CURL UP INTO A TIGHT BALL?

5. What word do humans use to describe our winter sleep?

6. What do we hedgehogs like to eat? Do we like,
A) PLANTS AND FLOWERS?
B) SLUGS and WORMS? or
C) SNAILS and BEETLES?

7. What could you feed me or any other hedgehog in your garden? Which of these could you put out for me?
A) BREAD & MILK?
B) CAT OR DOG FOOD IN JELLY (NOT GRAVY)?
C) CAT BISCUITS?
D) MEALWORMS?
E) WATER TO DRINK?

8. On average how long do we hedgehogs live in the wild? Do we live,
A) 1-2YRS?
B) 3-5YRS? or
C) 6-10YRS?

9. What are baby hedgehogs called? Are they called
A) URCHINS?
B) KITTENS?
C) HOGLETS? or
D) CUBS?

10. Can we hedgehogs swim?
A) YES
B) NO
C) WE CAN FLOAT A BIT.

11. Is it a good idea to keep a hedgehog as a pet?
A) YES?
B) NO?
C) ONLY ONES FROM A PET SHOP?

Answers to Lucky the Hedgehog's Fun Facts Quiz

1. A) There are about only about 1 MILLION hedgehogs left in Great Britain.
2. Creatures that come out at night to feed like hedgehogs include: OWLS, BATS, BADGERS, FOXES, MICE, MOLES, MOTHS, SLUGS, BEETLES, SNAILS.
3. On average we hedgehogs have, A) 5000-7000 spines.
4. To protect ourselves C) WE CURL UP INTO A TIGHT BALL. Cats and Foxes will leave us alone but badgers and some AGGRESSIVE DOGS will attack us!
5. In winter we hedgehogs **hibernate** in a warm nest. Did you read about these superpowers in the notes?
6. We Hedgehogs like to eat B) SLUGS and WORMS and C) SNAILS and BEETLES
7. You can put the following out for me. B) cat or dog food in jelly (NOT GRAVY) C) cat biscuits D) mealworms and E) clean water to drink
8. We hedgehogs tend to live B) 3-5YRS in the wild.
9. Baby hedgehogs are called? C) HOGLETS is the

commonly used name nowadays. A) Urchins was the name given to us in the past: even Shakespeare mentions us.

10. A) YES we hedgehogs can swim BUT we need a slope or a ramp to scramble out otherwise we may drown.

11. B) NO it is definitely not a good idea to keep a hedgehog as a pet for the reasons given below:-

i)   We are wild animals.
ii) We need to forage for food.
iii) We can be very smelly.
iv) We often have fleas. Thankfully our fleas do not affect cats, dogs or humans.
v)   We get stressed very easily.
vi) We are not easy to handle because our spines are so prickly.
vii) We sleep during the day which is when you might want to play with us.
viii) It is illegal to keep wild animals without a licence.